Three Little Words

Three Little Words

Words

Love
Unexpected
a romance compilation

Jennie Hansen,
K.C. Grant,
& Aubrey Mace

Covenant Communications, Inc.

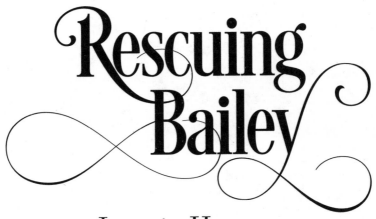

Rescuing Bailey

Jennie Hansen

For my granddaughters, Kate, McKayla, Alena,
Jennifer, and Gracie

Also a special thank you to Mindi, Maridean, and Janice for
their support and encouragement

Chapter One

I NEED MY HEAD EXAMINED! It was all Bailey could do to move her feet one after the other. Thick mud clung to her legs, and a loud slurping sound accompanied each lift of her feet. Dark splatters dotted her arms and face, and her shorts and shirt would probably never be clean again. *I must have been out of my mind when I agreed to this!* This wasn't her first triathlon, but it was one of the hardest she'd undertaken. From now on, she'd stick to plain old marathons.

It's only two hundred feet, she reminded herself. She'd stayed ahead of the pack during the swim across the lake, and the bicycle leg of the race had ended neck and neck. She'd hit the mud portion of the run before the next competitor, but maintaining her slight lead wasn't going well. The mud wasn't the thin, watery sort she'd expected; it was thick ooze that pulled at her legs and sucked at the last dregs of her energy. She hadn't had a chance to train properly for this type of competition.

"Ooh!" Sharp pain stabbed the back of her right knee, and she began to slide. It felt like someone had kicked her. Her arms flailed in a windmill motion as she struggled to regain her balance. Stacy Cornwell staggered abreast of her as gravity and slippery, thick mud combined to topple Bailey to her knees. A quick tug on her ponytail startled her, causing her to lose her precarious balance. Fortunately Bailey had just enough presence of mind to hold her breath as her face struck the disgusting brown muck. *Did Stacy knock me down on purpose? It wouldn't be the first time she's sabotaged one of my competitions to make herself look better.* They'd competed all through high school, not only in sports but for Dieter Morgan, Bailey's longtime boyfriend, as well. Stacy was the only child of wealthy, influential parents, which seemed to lead her to think she was entitled to anything she wanted.

Two more competitors, one of whom was Kathy Stevens, Bailey's old high school running partner, squished their way past her as she struggled to regain her footing and claim fourth place. She and Kathy had once been close but had drifted apart after they'd chosen to attend different colleges. Bailey had gone to Boston, while Kathy had stayed in Utah at Cedar City's SUU. Kathy's negative attitude toward Dieter had played a part too. She'd resented the amount of time Bailey had spent with him and claimed Bailey didn't know him as well as she thought she did. But to Kathy's credit, it had been she, in what Bailey considered an effort to reestablish their friendship, who had called and insisted that Bailey run in their Hopewell hometown triathlon for old-time's sake since she was finished with school and hadn't started a job. Bailey hadn't mentioned that the only reason she hadn't accepted a job offer yet was because she expected a proposal from Dieter any day. Their graduations, on opposite sides of the country, were just two weeks ago, and they'd seen each other almost every day since returning to Utah.

Standing alone at the finish line, Bailey raked a hand across her begrimed face in a futile attempt to remove the generous coating of mud. Her shoulders slumped. It would do no good to accuse Stacy of deliberately hitting her, though she had no doubt that was the case. Stacy lacked ethics, but she was clever and rarely got caught. Bailey looked around again, growing increasingly concerned. There was no sign of Kathy either. Bailey had been looking forward to getting together with her longtime friend after the race, but now she suspected she'd been set up.

Where is Dieter? He promised he'd meet me at the finish line. He'd been jittery and nervous when he'd asked Bailey to walk with him the previous evening, but they'd gotten no farther than the oak that separated their backyards. She'd thought he might ask the big question and that was the reason he wasn't his usual smooth, confident self. Instead he'd pleaded a headache and promised to meet her after the race.

"Bailey!"

She turned, her hopes rising . . . then plummeting when she saw only Dieter's younger brother, Gunter, hurrying toward her. Gunter had a knack for showing up when Bailey was expecting Dieter. She'd come to resent him when all too often he'd shown up in Dieter's place when Dieter had changed his mind, was running late, or had become involved in something other than their planned activity.

Gunter was a good friend, and they were the same age, but it was two-years-older and handsomer Dieter who made her heart pound.

She had been in love with him since she was six years old and he and his family had moved in next door. They'd met when her kitten had climbed the large tree in front of her house and she'd gone up after it only to get stuck. Her shoe had slipped, then gotten caught where a thick limb branched out from the tree trunk, leaving her dangling by one foot. As she'd screamed for help, a boy had dashed around the far side of the neighboring house and stood grinning beneath her for long seconds before reaching for the lowest branch to pull himself up so he was level with her upside-down face. He'd said something she hadn't understood, but she'd guessed he'd asked if she was all right. Later she'd learned the family had recently arrived from Germany and only their father spoke any English.

Dizziness had come with her upside-down position, and before she could answer, she became aware of a second boy, who had also climbed the tree and was perched higher up, near her trapped foot. She felt a tug on her foot and felt her shoe fly off, then she fell headfirst, unable to stop herself. The next thing she knew, she was lying on the ground looking up at two scared boys. The taller one held her kitten in his arms, and the smaller one dangled her shoe from one hand. The younger one, who she later learned was Gunter, dropped her shoe and ran to his house. Moments later, an excited woman arrived, and though Bailey didn't understand a word the woman said, she did understand she was sending Gunter to fetch Bailey's mother. Twelve years passed before she learned Dieter had scared the cat up the tree in the first place.

As Gunter approached her at the finish line, he didn't have his customary grin in place. She'd seldom seen him angry, but now he reminded her of her dad's descriptive phrase "mad enough to chew nails." She wasn't certain whether he was merely disappointed in the outcome of the race or was upset over once again having to rescue her. "Come on. I'll show you where the showers are." He reached for her arm, but before he could touch her, she drew back.

"Don't get too close, or you'll be covered in mud too," she warned.

"I don't care." He took her arm in spite of her objections, and she had little choice but to follow his lead. As they wove their way through the crowd, people stepped back as soon as they saw her. Some murmured words of sympathy. A few snickered, and others merely looked concerned about avoiding contact.

Just as they reached the area set up for the race participants to shower, the loud speaker squawked to announce the trophy ceremony. Bailey couldn't help glancing back. She should have been on that platform. Instead she watched Stacy mount the stage, already hosed off and wearing clean shorts and shoes. Bailey did a double take when she saw Dieter—her Dieter—escorting Stacy and Stacy clinging to him the way her wet T-shirt was clinging to her curves. Then Bailey's world stopped, and her mouth dropped open when Dieter bent to kiss Stacy's lips before stepping back beside the escorts for the second- and third-place winners.

Kathy wore a triumphant smile as she high-fived Stacy, who in turn directed a smirk in Bailey's direction.

Shock slammed through Bailey like she'd been physically punched. She couldn't see or think. She couldn't even cry. Earlier, she'd noticed the huge diamond on Stacy's left hand, and she'd wondered at Dieter's awkwardness the last few times they'd been together. Her suspicions about Kathy's motive in calling her became real; Kathy and Stacy had concocted this plan to humiliate her and make certain she knew of Stacy's claim to Dieter.

She was vaguely aware of Gunter's arms encircling her and of being rocked back and forth while he whispered in her ear. "I'm so sorry. If I'd known . . . Being just two states away, he's come home far more often than you have, and he's been dating Stacy each time he's come home for almost a year. She's flown to California to be with him several times as well. I should have told you, but I waited for him to break it to you."

At last, she wrenched free and disappeared inside the makeshift shower stall. Her legs threatened to collapse. The canvas walls of the temporary shower provided no place to lean her head. She could only hold it between her hands as, at last, the tears came, mixing with the stream of water meant to wash away the mud that clung to every inch of her body and hair. She watched the grime slide off of her and felt her hopes and dreams go with it.

She and Dieter had started dating when they were in high school, and she'd begun almost at once fantasizing about marriage and a family after Dieter finished law school and she graduated from college with a business degree. Just two weeks ago, their graduation ceremonies had conflicted, hers in Boston and his in Palo Alto, three thousand miles apart, but their reunion at the airport had been all she'd dreamed. She'd expected a formal proposal any minute since then.

She'd heard rumors on her infrequent trips home during the past two years that Dieter was dating other girls, and since she'd returned following graduation, even her sister, Jamie, had tried to warn her that he was dating someone else. Blinded by her feelings for Dieter, she'd refused to listen. Dismissing Jamie's words was easy. Being eight years older than Bailey, Jamie didn't really know Bailey's friends, and Bailey had long outgrown any need for the perpetual, self-appointed babysitter Jamie had been as long as Bailey could remember. But seeing Stacy with Dieter and their easy familiarity suggested their year together had been more than friendly.

The lukewarm water turned cold, and Bailey realized she was shivering. There were no towels in the small area, so she had no choice but to leave the cubicle, looking like a drowned rat. She peeked through the curtain to where Gunter was standing a short distance away with his back to her. Seeing her chance to escape unseen, she darted behind the curtain and fled across the park. She found her car, unearthed her keys from her pocket, and drove home as fast as she dared. The following morning, she was on a plane to Chicago to accept a job offer she hadn't previously even considered.

Chapter Two

Bailey picked up her desk phone with one hand and continued studying the facts on the report she'd prepared for the board meeting. "Bailey Morris." The words were automatic, her attention still on the report.

"I'm sorry, Ms. Morris," the receptionist said. "I know you said you didn't want any calls until after the board meeting, but this gentleman is adamant; he must talk to you now."

"Did he give you his name?"

"Jim Cassady."

Jim Cassady! Her sister's husband. Her full attention shifted to the phone call. Jamie had recently announced she was expecting again. Bailey felt a shiver of apprehension. Could there be a problem with her sister? Had something gone wrong with the baby? "Put him through."

"Bailey?"

"What's going on, Jim?" She skipped the small talk. "Is it Jamie?"

"No, Jamie's fine. It's your dad. He had a heart attack a few hours ago. Jamie and your mom are at the hospital with him. I promised to let you know."

"Dad? How serious . . . ?"

"He was taken by ambulance to Cedar City, then Life-Flighted to Salt Lake. They think you should be here."

"I'll be there as soon as I can get a flight." Pain clutched at her heart. She and her father had always been close. They'd fished and camped together. He'd been there for all her ball games and track events, except that last horrible triathlon when he'd been out of town on a business trip. They'd shared the kind of adventures fathers usually shared with sons, and he'd never given her cause to suspect he regretted she wasn't the son he'd never had.

"All right. Let me know when, and I'll pick you up."

"You don't need to pick me up. I'll rent a car."

From the corner of her eye, she saw Chad Overfield poke his head around her doorjamb and signal for her to hurry. She hung up and turned to face him. Blinking back tears, she whispered, "I have to go home. It's my dad. My brother-in-law said he had a heart attack, and I'm needed there."

"I'm sorry, sweetie." He wrapped his arms around her. "Just as soon as this meeting is over, you should go straight to your apartment to pack. I'll drive you."

He released her to pick up her phone. "Carla, make reservations for Bailey Morris on the first flight you can get after four thirty to Salt Lake City." He paused and nodded, though his secretary couldn't see the gesture. "Reserve a rental car and put it all on the department's expense account."

"This is personal. I can pay," Bailey protested.

"We can discuss that later. Right now we need to get to the boardroom. Do you have everything you need?"

She reached for the folder she'd set on her desk only moments ago and fingered the thumb drive she'd prepared for Chad. She wasn't sure she could do this. She'd never been truly comfortable giving reports or speaking to groups, even with her high school experience on the declamation team, but she knew how important this was to Chad. She'd never expected to move up so quickly in a large corporation, and she owed a lot of her success to him. He'd taken her under his wing when she'd arrived at Smith, Finster & Davenport almost three years ago and had encouraged her to take on challenges and broaden her skills. Her business administration degree had come in handy, and promotions and raises had followed, the last one including her own office next to Chad's, overlooking the city she now considered home.

It had also been the beginning of a subtle shift in their relationship. At first they'd merely been coworkers who had helped each other when they could. When Chad was promoted to finance department head, she was given the opportunity to transfer with him and eventually became his chief assistant. Recently their relationship had become more personal, and Chad had dropped several hints concerning marriage. She couldn't think about that now. Nor could she let her concern for her father swamp her with worry. This meeting called for her professional best. Somehow she'd get through delivering the portion of the report Chad had requested she make before the executive officers. She'd been happy to do it for him, though it had entailed a lot of extra work. She'd spent the past two weeks preparing and fine-tuning every fact and figure concerning the company's marketing ventures.

Pasting a serene smile on her face, she stepped into the boardroom. She greeted the chairman, the company CEO, and several other executives on her way to the seat beside the one Chad had claimed. Though meetings such as this were always recorded for the various executives' secretaries' convenience, Bailey always took notes, finding it easier to pull up the information she needed from her own records than tracking down Carla's copy of the meetings' proceedings. Bailey set her PDA on the table and took her seat.

Several speakers droned on for much too long, and Bailey found her mind wandering. She should have gone home more often. At first, she didn't think she could risk the pain associated with her hometown and the announcement of Dieter's engagement to Stacy, but she'd been over her silly infatuation with him for a long time now. Knowing his parents lived next door to hers and she might accidentally run into him or Stacy anytime she visited her family wasn't a reasonable excuse for her to neglect those she loved. If her father survived this attack, she'd make it up to them. She didn't know how, but she would.

Fortunately Chad's presentation was announced, forcing her to push her guilt to the back of her mind. She was ready when he turned the microphone to her, and her worry about her dad eclipsed her fear of the meeting, allowing her to speak with poise and confidence—anything to be done and be on her way to her father's side. When she finished, Chad wrapped up his report and received a round of applause. She longed to rush from the room once her part was finished. The wait was agonizing through the last report and the chairman's final remarks.

The meeting finally ended, and Bailey moved as quickly as she could without appearing to rush from the room. Different people stopped her several times, wishing to congratulate her on her contribution to Chad's report. A couple hinted she'd be welcome to transfer to their departments. Ordinarily she would have been thrilled by the positive reception, but at the moment, she could only concentrate on reaching her father quickly.

Taking the elevator down one floor from the executive suite, Bailey bypassed her own office and hurried toward Chad's secretary. Whenever possible, she avoided spending any more time than she had to with Carla. The secretary was near Bailey's age, but there the resemblance ended. Carla was a petite, silvery blonde with a definite eye for fashion. It seemed the designers of stiletto heels and the latest trends created their wares with her in mind. Most people found her outgoing and friendly, but she'd always been distant and cool with Bailey. She'd suspected for some time that Carla resented her close working relationship with Chad, which could become a serious problem in the future if their relationship went as Bailey suspected it might, but at the moment, she was nowhere near ready to let anyone know she and Chad were dating, especially Carla.

"Carla," she kept her voice neutral as she approached the other woman's desk. "Were you able to book a flight for me?"

"Yes, of course, Miss Morris. I took the liberty of printing your boarding pass and calling a cab." She smiled and appeared almost friendly as she handed the papers to Bailey. There was to be a reception that evening to celebrate quotas met and promotions and to honor two retiring board members. Bailey suspected glamorous Carla was pleased Bailey wouldn't be attending.

Bailey glanced at the papers, then back at the elevator. Her flight left in a little over two hours. Chad was nowhere in sight, and she couldn't wait for him. If she was going to stuff a few clothes in a bag and make it to the airport in time to get through security, she had to leave immediately.

Chapter Three

HUDDLING IN HER SEAT WITH her eyes closed and without making a move to lift the blind covering the small window at her side, Bailey felt the big 747 lift off from O'Hare International Airport. Under normal circumstances, she was an avid flier who loved takeoffs and landings and watched every detail, but this time she only wanted the flight to pass quickly. She'd attempted to call Jim from the cab for an update on her father's condition but had been unable to reach him. She could only assume he was at the hospital with his phone turned off.

In an attempt to take her mind off her father, she turned her thoughts to Chad and wished he'd been able to drive her to the airport. When she'd first moved to Chicago, she'd given no thought to a romantic relationship with anyone. But over the past few weeks, she and Chad had worked closely on the presentation they'd given that afternoon and grown closer. She'd accompanied him to a number of formal dinners with executives of some of the company's subsidiaries. They'd pored over facts and figures until late at night at her apartment, and she'd worked even later compiling the numbers that had showcased the points Chad had wished to highlight for the executive board.

She frowned, remembering their argument two nights ago. He'd removed a section from the PowerPoint presentation that she thought showed an area where they could tighten their advertising expenditures. She wanted the presentation to show an awareness of all marketing aspects and to highlight cost-saving goals for improvement. Chad was equally adamant that the report only highlight achievements and showcase their successes.

It wasn't the first time she'd disagreed with him, but it was the first time she'd openly done so. She hadn't gotten her way because Chad was the department head and she resigned herself to following his lead. He hadn't reached his position by making poor choices, she assured herself. Too many late nights was the only excuse she could give for the argument, and though it hadn't been pleasant, it had had one positive twist. Without knowing quite how it had happened, she'd wound up in Chad's arms, and he'd kissed her. Maybe she wasn't as opposed to falling in love as she'd thought.

She wasn't certain whether she'd actually slept on the flight or just zoned out for a bit, but she was fully awake and anxious to reach her father's side when the plane landed. As soon as the seat belt signs were off, she climbed over her seat mates to reach the overhead bins, extracted her carry-on bag, and began working her way down the aisle. She received more than a few annoyed glares but hurried anyway.

Once she was free of the crowded gate, it was all she could do to keep from breaking into a run down the concourse to the baggage area, where she waited impatiently for her bag to appear. Just as she reached for it, another hand gripped the handle of her bag and pulled it from the carousel.

"That's—" She started to claim her bag but realized the man standing beside her with the bag now firmly gripped in his hand was Gunter. She hadn't seen him since she'd left him waiting outside the triathlon showers nearly three years ago.

"Hello." He grinned.

"Uh, hi." She certainly hadn't expected to see anyone she knew at the airport, especially her childhood playmate and good friend.

"Just the one bag?" he asked.

"Yes. I can take it from here." She reached to claim her bag.

"It's okay. I've got it, and it isn't far to my car."

"I arranged for a rental." She felt confused. Gunter talked like he'd purposely come for her, like it wasn't the chance meeting she'd presumed. A twinge of bitter memory reminded her of all the times he'd met her or taken her home when she'd expected Dieter. Of course she hadn't expected Dieter today, but she had no idea why Gunter had come for her either. The last time he'd seen her, she'd been covered from head to toe with mud, and she'd left him without a word of farewell. She was surprised he even recognized her in a designer suit, with her hair highlighted and much shorter.

"You look confused. You must not have received Jim's text informing you I'd meet your plane." He smiled the same grin she'd once seen on a daily basis. "I told him you were probably already in the air with your phone off. Your mother and sister are at the hospital and plan to stay the night at a nearby hotel. They got you a room too. You can cancel the car rental, and I'll drive you to either the hotel or the hospital, whichever you prefer first."

"Since I'll be staying in the city, I could just call a cab."

"No need. I was close when the ambulance picked up your father. When the Cedar City hospital arranged to fly him to the bigger hospital in Salt Lake, I volunteered to bring your mother into the city. We met Jim and Jamie at the hospital, and Jim mentioned you were flying in. Since I was available, I said I'd meet your flight."

That explained a lot. Gunter always had had a white-knight complex. Clearly he'd still not outgrown his penchant for rescuing her from dragons, but she really could have made her way to the hospital on her own. The less she had to do with any of the

Morgans, the better. If she'd thought about it, she should have realized her mother wouldn't make the three-hour drive back home tonight while her husband was in the hospital. Bailey was an adult. She wouldn't create a scene. If it killed her, she would be polite to Gunter, let him drive her to the hospital, then say good-bye, and never see him again.

The thought filled her with a twinge of sadness. More often than she cared to admit, she'd missed Gunter since she'd moved to Chicago.

Shoving the strap of her carry-on bag farther onto her shoulder, she followed Gunter to his car. Once they were on their way, she took a deep breath and asked, "Dad . . . Do you know . . . ? I suppose if you followed the ambulance, there probably isn't any word yet . . ."

Gunter placed a hand on hers. "It's serious, but the EMTs indicated his chances are good. Your family will probably know more by the time we get there." It wasn't the first time Gunter had touched her in a consoling gesture. She felt foolish now, remembering all the times he had apologized or attempted to console her because of his brother's inconsiderate behavior. She had to admit there was something comforting in the familiar gesture.

Sitting beside him as he drove wasn't as awkward as she'd expected. He'd been present for almost every major event during her growing-up years. It hadn't been until she'd realized how much she was in love with his brother that they'd grown apart. The last person she wanted to think about was Dieter. Redirecting her thoughts once again to her father, she asked, "How did you happen to be there when my father had the attack?"

"I noticed he was trimming that monster tree in the front yard when I came home from my run this morning. I told him I'd be over to help as soon as I changed my clothes. I was on my way back out when I heard your mother calling for help. She thought he'd fallen, but when I got there and saw him clutching his chest, I suspected it was his heart."

"You're living with your parents again?" So much for her plans to never see him again after he delivered her to the hospital.

"Not really. Dad has some business he needs to take care of in Germany, and it seemed like a good time to clear up some property that my mother's father left her. They expect to be gone at least six months. I moved back home to keep up the house and yard while they're gone."

"What about your job?"

"I have my own business now. What I can't do through remote computer access involves travel, so my home base can be anywhere."

"That must be nice." Her mind wandered to the sprawl of buildings they were approaching, and she recognized the Intermountain Medical Center. Gunter pulled smoothly into a parking spot on the east side of the largest building in the complex. Bailey took in the large sign that said *Emergency*, and fear and discouragement overwhelmed her. Gunter opened her door and took her hand, and they walked briskly toward a set of glass doors. She'd never been inside the big new hospital, and for just a moment, she was grateful Gunter knew the way. Then she saw Jamie and began to run, with Gunter scrambling to keep up.

Chapter Four

"DAD?" SHE UNTANGLED HER HAND from Gunter's and wrapped her arms around her sister, who returned her fierce hug.

"He's in the ICU now. The doctor said he did a double bypass and everything went well. Mom is with him. She sent us to wait for you."

Bailey hadn't been aware of Jim standing beside Jamie until just then. She turned to him. "Thank you for calling."

"You're welcome. I'm glad you were able to get a flight so quickly."

"I don't think they'll move Dad to his own room tonight. We should probably go back to the ICU waiting room." Jamie took Bailey's arm and led her down the hall toward the elevators. Jim and Gunter trailed behind. "Mom is having a hard time. They won't let her stay with Dad for more than a few minutes each hour, and I don't want her to be alone."

The moment they entered the waiting area, Bailey's mom rushed to gather her in her arms. "I'm so glad you're here. This has been the scariest day of my life. Your poor father has always been so strong and busy doing things. It's hard seeing him lying there, still and defenseless. I was so frightened when he collapsed,

I couldn't think. I don't know what I would have done if Gunter hadn't been there to help me." Bailey hugged her mother back and felt a surge of guilt for not being more gracious to Gunter.

It's just that all my life every time I've messed up—or been stood up—Gunter has been the one sent to look after poor me. I can't help associating him with every negative, embarrassing moment I've ever experienced.

"Here, dear." Her mother urged her toward a short sofa. "You must be exhausted after working all day, then your long flight."

"Mom, you probably need to rest more than I do." Her mother looked disheveled and exhausted, which was far from Ellen Morris's usual appearance. Even so, Bailey sank onto the stiff piece of furniture. She was exhausted, but she hoped she'd get to see her father for a few minutes, and she couldn't help worrying her mother would be ill too if she didn't get some rest.

"Mrs. Morris?" A nurse stood in the doorway. "You can see Dallas for a few minutes, then Dr. Chandler left instructions for you to get some rest. He doesn't want you to become a patient too."

"Oh, I can't—"

"Yes, Mom. As soon as you return from Dad's room, Jim and I will take you to your room," Jamie said. "Gunter and Bailey can stay here until we get back."

"You might as well get a few hours' sleep too," Gunter said to Jim. "I'm sure you'll want to check on your kids, and it can't be good for Jamie to get overtired. We'll be fine, and I'll call if anything changes."

When they left for the hotel, Bailey curled up on one end of the sofa and was almost asleep when the same nurse who had appeared earlier peeked in the door. "Are you Dallas Morris's daughter?" she asked.

"Yes, I'm Bailey Morris."

"Would you like to see your father for a few minutes?"

Bailey eagerly followed the nurse down a short hall, fully awake now. She scrubbed carefully and donned a hospital gown before being ushered into a room dominated by machines that made strange sounds. Taking slow, hesitant steps, she approached the bed. She stood with one hand braced on the metal railing and looked at the man who had been her strength for as long as she could remember. Wires and tubes connected him to machines, making him barely recognizable.

"Daddy. I love you." The words came out in a hoarse whisper.

His eyes flickered open, and she thought he attempted to smile before they closed again. Somehow that small gesture filled her with hope and brought a fresh sheen of moisture to her eyes.

Too soon, the nurse escorted her back to the waiting room. Gunter's eyes, filled with concern, met hers. His arms circled her shoulders, and he led her back to the small sofa. She didn't protest when he sat beside her and pulled her against his chest. The tears she'd fought since Jim's call ran down her cheeks. Gunter held her while she cried. Eventually the tears stopped, and the long day, with all its stress and worry, gave way to sleep, and Gunter continued to hold her.

Bailey awoke as the first rays of morning streamed through the waiting room window. She lay sprawled against Gunter, with her head resting against his chest. His head was back, and he half lay, half sat on the too-small sofa, holding her in a secure grip. She lay still for several minutes, worrying that if she moved, he'd awaken. She preferred he not know she'd slept for hours in his arms. Chagrin filled her as she admitted to herself another reason to not move: she was perfectly comfortable where she was.

The sound of footsteps approaching changed her mind. She could not endure one more embarrassing episode with Gunter, and she couldn't face having her mother and sister find her plastered against him.

"Gunter! Wake up," she hissed as she struggled to disentangle herself from him.

"What? Huh?" He stretched and smoothly moved to an upright position. When he'd come to enough to register his surroundings, a wicked smile flitted across his face, leaving her wondering if he'd been as oblivious to their position as she'd thought.

Chapter Five

"But, Mom . . ." What was the use? They'd rotated between the hotel and the hospital for three days, and Bailey knew perfectly well her mother wouldn't leave her dad long enough to return to her house. Jamie had two preschool-age children she couldn't leave for long periods, and Jim couldn't take any more time off work than necessary. That left Bailey to make the trek, ensure all was well at home, and prepare the house for her father's return. The only part she objected to was traveling with Gunter and being dependent on him for transportation back to Salt Lake when the time came to return to Chicago. Her whole family and Gunter acted like she'd proposed robbing a bank when she'd said she'd rent a car. She expelled a long breath. She might as well accept the inevitable.

Actually, she and Gunter had been getting along quite well since her arrival in Salt Lake. It had been easy and natural to fall back into their old camaraderie. He made frequent trips to the hotel or his car to use his laptop or phone but was always around at mealtimes to insist she visit the cafeteria, or he brought snacks to share with her. They reminisced about their school days and caught up on their respective careers.

Her father was making excellent progress, according to Dr. Chandler, and would soon be released from the hospital. The doctor suggested her mother rent a hospital bed for her husband and cautioned that he should avoid stairs until he became stronger. That meant Dallas's den had to be turned into a bedroom, and Bailey was the logical person to make the necessary changes.

Dallas was out of the ICU now but was still being closely monitored in the cardiac unit. When Bailey went in to visit him, she explained she'd be leaving shortly to prepare for his homecoming. He seemed concerned until she mentioned she'd be with Gunter. She felt a flash of annoyance that even her dad seemed to think she needed Gunter to look after her. On the other hand, it was great to see her father returning to his old take-charge self.

Gunter's car had comfortable seats and air conditioning for the three-hour ride back to Hopewell. Conversation seemed to flow without effort, and Gunter seemed genuinely interested in Bailey's job and her life in Chicago. An uneasy thought crossed her mind: why hadn't Chad called? Of course, she'd been in the hospital with her phone turned off much of the time since arriving in Salt Lake, and there was a time difference, but he could have left a message, she thought, annoyed.

She felt the car begin to slow, and she looked up to see they were approaching the Hopewell exit. A strange sense of anticipation filled her. Her family wouldn't be there, but it felt good to be returning to her hometown. She had a lot of happy memories linked to that small place where she'd grown up.

Gunter pulled into his driveway and stopped beside a bright-yellow sports car. Bailey's heart sank. She hoped the car didn't signify Dieter had come to visit his brother. It was the flashy kind of car he'd drive. She wasn't ready to see him again, and she might not ever be. Gunter pulled her bag from the trunk and carried it across their connecting front lawns to her door without mentioning the car or its owner. She fumbled to open the door and was relieved to step inside the familiar walls.

Gunter followed, setting her bag on the thick carpet. "Rest for a little while," he suggested. "Your mother said the hospital bed won't be delivered until tomorrow morning. I'll be over in a couple hours to help you move anything heavy to make room for it."

Resting was the last thing she planned to do. Getting the den rearranged and the house spotless were her first priorities. She had no intention of wasting time getting started.

She thanked Gunter for bringing her home and closed the door behind him before turning to survey the room. It hadn't changed much since she was little. Except for a strange odor. Suspecting the foul smell came from the kitchen, she hurried in that direction. An open can of tuna fish, shelled boiled eggs, a dry loaf of bread, moldy strawberries, and a couple of overripe bananas sat beside two glasses of curdled milk on the island separating the kitchen from the breakfast nook. No doubt the warm days without the air conditioner running had helped their self-destruction. A skillet sat on a burner, telling Bailey her Mom had been preparing to grill tuna sandwiches for lunch when her dad had collapsed. Thank goodness, her mom hadn't left a burner on.

Gathering the spoiled food, she carried it outside to the trash can, then returned to open a window. For good measure, she sprayed air freshener throughout the downstairs rooms. With that task finished, she carried her bag upstairs to her old room.

For just a moment, she expected to see the refuge of her teenage years before she remembered her mom had long ago turned her room into a guest room and Jamie's room into her sewing/craft room. Fortunately her mother had kept Jamie's old daybed in her sewing room so there would be a place for the girls to sleep when they visited. Bailey's old room was lovely but impersonal. The posters and trophies had been put away. Her eyes went to the bedside table where she'd expected to see a photo of Dieter and her taken at her junior prom and that had greeted her every morning as soon as she'd opened her eyes when she'd lived here, but in its place sat a small lamp and a box of tissues. An oil landscape some distant cousin had painted hung on the wall, and a thick apple-green comforter and drapes had replaced the bold orange and blue stripes that had once graced the room.

Everything in there suited the professional woman she'd become much better now. Anyway, she didn't have time to think about the past if she was going to have everything ready for her father's arrival the next day. She unpacked her suitcase and shoved it into the closet. Next, she changed into jeans and a T-shirt.

Just as she was trying to decide whether she should try calling Chad, a sound drew her to the window. Knowing the view overlooked the Morgans' driveway and remembering the yellow car parked there, she took care to remain where the curtains hid her should anyone glance up in her direction.

Just as she feared, Dieter stood beside the sports car, leaning against the open door, with Gunter a short distance away. Bailey's stomach did an odd twist. The fluttery feeling in her stomach that once marked Dieter's arrival was gone. In its place was something closer to nausea. The two men appeared to be arguing, though she couldn't hear anything either of them was saying. Finally Dieter climbed into his car and backed out of the driveway with a loud roar. Gunter glanced up toward her window before disappearing back inside his house. She was glad she'd taken the precaution of staying out of sight.

Sinking down on a low chair, she tried to analyze the confusion of feelings that raced through her on seeing Dieter. Of one thing she was sure: she was no longer in love with him. He was an important part of her past, but it was embarrassing to recall how she'd let her infatuation overrule good sense. How had she tolerated the cavalier way he'd stood her up or sent her home with Gunter when having her around interfered with something else he wanted to do? How could she have been so spineless?

In an odd sort of way, it was a relief to know Dieter no longer mattered to her. Too much of her time had been wasted watching him and pondering his place in her life. Anger swept through her, giving her the energy to jump to her feet and rush down-stairs. She worked like a madwoman to transfer books and chairs to other rooms. Several times she eyed the computer resting on the desk and finally set to work disconnecting it. Her parents didn't use it a lot, but her dad occasionally checked ball-game scores or researched genealogy on it. The desk was too heavy and awkward to move alone though. She'd have to accept Gunter's help moving that. Fortunately the sofa converted into a bed, since there was no way her mother would consider sleeping upstairs in their room and leaving her husband alone downstairs.

Gunter arrived sooner than Bailey had expected and pitched in at once. Working together, it didn't take long to move the heavy oak desk into the dining room, where it would still be accessible but out of the way. Then they started putting the computer back together.

"Hand me that USB cable." Gunter didn't look up as he worked, and Bailey felt a twinge of annoyance as she handed him the cord. *Why do men assume I'm only capable of handing them tools or parts as needed?* She could have set up the computer and connected the printer as easily, and maybe more quickly, than Gunter had. No, that wasn't true. Honesty compelled her to admit that with Gunter's help the task was taking a remarkably short time, and he wasn't pretending to know more than she did.

When they finished, Gunter leaned back in her dad's office chair and asked, "How about going out to dinner with me? You've worked hard, and you must be awfully tired of hospital cafeteria food."

They'd eaten together for three days, but somehow that was different from the invitation he'd just extended. They really hadn't had much choice. But to go to one of the four restaurants in town together would invite gossip; people who had known her and her family all of her life were sure to see them. They might even bump into Dieter and Stacy. "No, I'm awfully tired. I'll just fix a quick bite here and soak in the tub before making it an early night."

For just a moment, Gunter appeared disappointed, or did she imagine that? His smile returned quickly though, and he wished her a good night.

Strangely, she felt a perverse disappointment when he walked out the door without trying to change her mind.

Chapter Six

EVERYTHING WAS AS READY AS she could get it for her father's return, at least until the rental company delivered the hospital bed the next morning. A sandwich would do for dinner, then a long soak in the bathtub would complete her evening. Her tiny bathroom back in Chicago had only a shower, making the prospect of a long, steamy bath particularly appealing. Before heading for the big, claw-foot tub upstairs, she checked her phone for messages.

Nothing. Chad should have found time to call by now. She debated calling him. On the chance he might have a dinner appointment with a client, she decided to send a short text telling him her dad was doing well and that he could expect her back at the office in about a week. Then she headed upstairs.

Leaning back in the deep tub now, she sighed in appreciation. It seemed like forever since she'd enjoyed the luxury of a bubble bath. In fact, it seemed like more than forever since she'd felt so relaxed.

She awoke with a start. The water was cold, the bubbles were gone, and her phone was ringing. Scrambling out of the tub, she snatched her phone from the counter. "Hello." She was too late; the caller had given up.

A wave of disappointment washed over her, and she quickly checked to see who had called, hoping Chad was trying to get in touch with her. She didn't recognize the number, but the area code was local. It wasn't Chad. It was probably a wrong number or one of the neighbors wondering about her father. She wouldn't try calling back. It was late, and it would be better to go to bed.

* * *

Morning came with a burst of song from a pair of birds she suspected were building a nest in the apricot tree outside her window. Donning a pair of sweatpants and a T-shirt, she hurried outside, assuring herself there would be plenty of time for a run before the delivery truck arrived. She seldom had a chance to run outdoors in Chicago, though she often ran on an indoor track at a gym near her apartment. Somehow it just wasn't the same.

Starting out at a walk, she covered the first block before breaking into a slow jog. Gradually picking up speed, she left the paved street for a winding dirt road that made its way up a mountain canyon. The sun felt good on her back, and she loved to breathe the clean mountain air. A sense of well-being she hadn't experienced for a long time wiped away the past days' somber mood.

She was almost two miles up the canyon when she heard footsteps pounding up the trail behind her. Panic struck, and she struggled to pick up her pace. She wasn't in Chicago, but that city didn't have a corner on psychos who preyed on females they found alone. Her sporadic workouts at the gym hadn't kept her speed up, and she doubted she could outrun a determined pursuer.

The steps drew closer, and a voice called out, "I thought I'd find you here."

"Gunter!" She shouldn't have been surprised that he'd followed her. When they'd been in high school, they'd run together almost every morning. Though he hadn't been into running marathons or competing in track, as she had, he'd played both football and basketball and had considered a daily run essential training.

As he drew even with her, she glanced his way and felt a flutter all the way from her chest to her toes. She didn't remember Gunter possessing such beautifully defined muscles. He was a sight to behold. Back in high school, she could easily outrun him, but now she wasn't sure that would be possible. She wasn't sure she'd even want to try.

What was she thinking? The man beside her was Gunter! Good old Gunter, inventor of dragons and magic swords!

They ran only a short distance farther before Bailey announced she was turning back. "They're supposed to deliver the bed this morning, and my family will be here with Dad sometime today too. I need to be home for the delivery and to have lunch ready."

"Okay." Gunter turned back as well.

"You don't need to cut your run short too." Bailey told him.

"You'll need help positioning the bed."

Their steps fell into the same easy stride as when they'd run together as teenagers. A block before they reached their houses, they slowed to a walk. Bailey noticed Gunter was quieter than usual. Several times he seemed about to say something, then would change his mind. When they reached her front gate, she turned to face him. "Out with it. You have something on your mind; why don't you just say it?"

"It's . . . well . . . I really don't want . . . Dieter wants to talk to you. He says he didn't get a chance to explain before you ran off to Chicago."

"There's nothing to explain. He chose Stacy and the support her father could give his political aspirations." She didn't want to have this conversation, and she absolutely did not want to talk to or about Dieter. Dieter and Stacy had been married for more than two years, and she had nothing to say to either of them. Their time together was over. Done. Finished. She turned toward the house. Gunter followed. As she reached for the door, he reached for her elbow.

"Bailey, wait a minute. You don't have to speak to Dieter if you don't want to, but you might explain why you left without telling me good-bye."

Long-ago anger boiled to the surface. "I was just so tired of Dieter asking me out and me ending up with you when he changed his mind, of him changing his plans and you conveniently arriving to take me back home, of you being the one to cheer at my track meets instead of him. He said he loved me, then had no qualms about dumping me in your lap. And you let him! You always did whatever he told you to do. I was embarrassed by being treated like a child you had to look out for. When are you going to stop being his lackey?"

She jerked her arm free and opened the door. As she slammed it behind her, she thought she heard Gunter say, "I didn't do it for him."

Chapter Seven

ONLY THE FACT THAT SHE was waiting for the delivery of the hospital bed and hoping for a phone call kept her shower short. It took a great deal of self-discipline to shut out thoughts of Dieter and Gunter. If only Chad would call, she'd feel much better. She dressed in jeans and a T-shirt before preparing a bowl of cold cereal, then poured the milk and noted they were almost out. She'd need to restock the kitchen with a few essentials as soon as her father was settled in his new room.

It was almost noon when the phone rang. Since it was the house phone, she knew it wasn't Chad calling. It was Jamie, calling to say they were getting ready to leave the hospital. "Jim has gone to the pharmacy to get a couple prescriptions, then he's going to pick up the girls from his mother's. Mom's downstairs signing papers and checking Dad out, so we should be there in a few hours."

"The bed hasn't arrived, but everything else is ready," Bailey told her sister.

"I'm sure it'll be there soon." Jamie sounded exhausted.

After hanging up the phone, Bailey paced the floor and peered out the front window. She'd call the rental company if she knew which one to call, but Jim had made the arrangements, so all she could do was wait.

She decided to get on her dad's computer. She'd berated herself many times for leaving her laptop at her apartment in her rush to get to the airport, but with a few minutes to spare, she opened her e-mail account. Several messages were advertising. No matter how many times she blocked the senders, each day a few ads masquerading as messages somehow got through. She deleted them. There were messages from a couple of friends, but one particular sender caught her attention. She couldn't imagine why Chad's secretary was sending an e-mail to her personal account, but she clicked on it and began to read.

Bailey, I assume you know by now that Chad has been promoted to area manager over the southeastern states and begins his new assignment June 1. He'll be gone before you return. Did he tell you he is also getting married to Amanda Davenport, one of the owners' daughter? It was announced along with his promotion at the executive party a few hours after you left to be with your father. He didn't bother to tell me. I found out from the minutes I typed up the next morning. You and I haven't been close, but I can see now that that was Chad's doing. I suspect he played both of us and perhaps Amanda too, to reach the upper circle professionally. Without the presentation he gave the day you left, which was composed entirely of work you and I did, I doubt he would have gotten the promotion. I think you have a good chance of getting his old job here. If you do, I'd love to be your secretary, but if you'd prefer someone else, that's okay. I can't think of anyone I'd rather see than you control Chad's budget.

Carla Steinfelt

Could it be true? Bailey wasn't sure she could trust Carla, but what other reason could there be for receiving no calls or messages from Chad? Had he really manipulated Carla and her into doing his work and promoted jealousy between them to keep them from comparing notes? She hated to think she might have been that gullible again.

The persistent ringing of the doorbell interrupted her thoughts, reminding her of the delivery she was awaiting. With the flick of a button, the screen went blank, and she nearly tipped her chair over in her rush to reach the door. Could life get any worse?

She opened the door, and Gunter, with his back to her, turned his head far enough to give her a grin before carrying one end of the bed past her and into the den-turned-bedroom. Trailing behind him and one delivery man were Dieter and another delivery company employee balancing the mattress between them. Bringing up the rear was Stacy carrying a small box Bailey assumed held the controls for the bed.

Chaos reigned as everyone struggled to squeeze the components for the bed through the den door and position them advantageously. Bailey was returning from the upstairs linen closet with sheets for the bed when the front door opened again to reveal her father leaning heavily on Jim. Her mom fluttered behind them, and Jamie brought up the rear, with both children dancing around her, threatening to make a run for the backyard in their excitement over finally reaching their grandparents' home.

Bailey shoved the sheets into Stacy's hands, since she was the closest person with empty hands, and rushed to hug her father. With her brother-in-law's help, she guided him to his recliner.

"The bed was just delivered," she said apologetically, "so it isn't made up yet. I'll do that now."

"I'm fine right here." Dallas leaned back in his chair. "I've been stuck in bed long enough."

"Now, dear, you mustn't get overtired." Ellen fussed around, making certain Dallas was comfortable. She looked as though she needed a nap as much as her husband did.

"What am I supposed to do with this?" Stacy whined as though she'd never seen bedsheets before.

Bailey reached for the sheets but was interrupted before she could reclaim them.

"You'll need to sign this form." One of the delivery men thrust a clipboard in front of her.

"Do you gots any peanut butter?" Three-year-old Lisa tugged at Bailey's pants and looked hopeful. "Just a minute, honey. I have to write on this paper." She quickly scribbled her name. When she turned back to the child, she saw her disappearing into the kitchen with her sister, Ashley.

The doorbell rang. Stacy set the sheets on the first available surface as though glad to have an excuse to get rid of them and hurried to the door. When she opened it, a smiling neighbor stood there with a steaming casserole held firmly in her oven-mitted hands. Stacy sweetly thanked the neighbor, then turned to ask Bailey where she wanted Mrs. Olsen to set the casserole.

"On the kitchen counter," she managed to say before the doorbell rang again. Torn between answering the door and making her dad's bed, she hesitated. With Stacy still in the kitchen with Mrs. Olsen, Bailey sent Dieter to the door. He looked startled but went. Moments later, he returned with a large basket of rolls. She pointed to the kitchen.

There was no time to dwell on the fact that she was seeing Dieter up close against her will. Too many people running in and out created a lot of noise and confusion. Bailey could barely think and felt certain the situation couldn't be good for her father. The children needed to be fed. Probably everyone was in need of lunch, and she hadn't had time to get it ready. Someone needed to establish some order so Dad could rest. Jamie could generally be counted on to take charge, but the poor pregnant woman looked overwhelmed and had every reason to be too tired to take the responsibility today. If no one else was willing to take charge, Bailey supposed she'd have to do so herself. It seemed to be the only way she'd get the bed made.

"Jamie, would you take over in the kitchen and make sure everyone gets some lunch? Stacy, you know everyone; would you and Dieter please take charge of answering the door?"

Her small nieces appeared in the kitchen doorway. Lisa was lugging the peanut butter jar, and Ashley had a precarious hold on a loaf of frozen bread.

"Once the girls have eaten their lunch, I'll put them down for a nap." Jamie ushered her small daughters back into the kitchen. "I'll fix plates for Mom and Dad, then arrange a buffet-style lunch for everyone else."

"Be sure to eat something yourself, and joining the girls for a nap might be a good idea," Bailey told her sister.

Dieter ushered the delivery men out the door, and Bailey looked around for Jim and Gunter but didn't see them. Instead she noticed the exhaustion on her father's face and the weary droop to her mother's shoulders. Getting their beds made became her priority once again. She hurried to the newly improvised bedroom and was surprised to find Gunter and Jim just finishing tucking the last corners of the bedding in place.

She gave silent thanks that two people in the household had accomplished something useful without being prompted. She'd known for years that her brother-in-law was a good man to have around, but she was now ready to admit what she had known deep down for a long time: Gunter was much the same kind of man.

Chapter Eight

ONCE HER PARENTS WERE SETTLED in their new bedroom and Jamie was lying with her small daughters upstairs, Bailey sent Jim to the store with a shopping list for needed basics. Stacy took one look at the pile of dishes in the sink and found something she needed to do at the Morgans' house, and Bailey had no idea why Dieter and Gunter didn't go with her.

From the kitchen window where she stood rinsing dishes before placing them in the dishwasher, she could see Dieter and Gunter standing beside the old swing set in the backyard. Once again their gestures and body language suggested they were arguing. She hoped it wasn't for the same reason as their earlier argument. She'd discovered today that she could tolerate being around Dieter, but she still had no desire for a private chat with him. She'd been surprised by Dieter's and Stacy's arrival this afternoon and had taken care to give Dieter no opportunity to catch her alone.

She was almost grateful for the flurry of activity that had kept her too busy to dwell on her old relationship or her more recent one with Chad. It would be easy to question her own shortcomings, which must have played a part in her being dumped by the only two men she'd cared about and with whom she'd considered marriage.

What happened to polite partings based on unsuitability? Both men had gone behind her back to propose to other women. Both men had chosen women from influential families who could further their careers. Dieter had publicly humiliated her. Chad had used her skills and expertise for his own advancement.

Hurt and anger nearly blinded her now that she had time to think about it. She rubbed the back of her hand across her eyes and decided it was just tears blinding her. But the tears made her angrier. She wouldn't cry. Neither Dieter nor Chad was worth crying over. Grabbing a dishtowel, she scrubbed at her eyes. No way would she let anyone catch her crying over either of those jerks!

She pushed a button to turn on the dishwasher, then returned to a sink full of pans. There were plenty of casseroles for the evening meal, and Jim would return soon with milk. Thank goodness, she wouldn't have to worry about what to fix for dinner. Her thoughts turned to the e-mail Carla had sent. Should she apply for the manager position of her department? If she applied for it, it couldn't be to take revenge on Chad for using her expertise, then abandoning her. It had to be because she really wanted the job. But did she?

While growing up, she'd dreamed of a life that included a husband, children, involvement with her children's school, activity in her church, and continuing her interest in sports. Though she had a degree in business administration, she'd minored in athletics. Being back in Hopewell, she was reminded of how little time her life in Chicago left for physical activity. She hadn't run outdoors in Chicago except for one awkward stumble on the beach, and she hadn't skied since the winter before that. Today's run had reminded her of how much satisfaction she'd once gotten from challenging her physical abilities.

"Could we talk?"

"Ouch!" Bailey smacked her head against the side of the cupboard. She hadn't heard Dieter reenter the house through the back door. Gritting her teeth, she turned to face him. Whether she wanted it or not, it appeared she was destined to talk with Dieter.

"I've thought about it a lot, and I think I owe you an apology."
You think!

"Gunter insists it was my fault you left so abruptly after the triathlon. I know we talked about marriage before I left for law school, but I didn't think either of us took that seriously, and we dated others while we finished college."

He'd dated; she hadn't. Bailey was tempted to throw the dish towel at him. By the smallest margin, she refrained.

"It must have been something Gunter said or did. Stacy and I were both disappointed you fell and weren't on the platform with us that day for our big announcement. We expected you'd be excited and happy that two of your best friends were marrying each other. Our plan was to surprise you and share our happiness with you."

And if I believe that, I might be in the market for some beachfront property in Arizona. Bailey stared at Dieter. He seemed to believe his own revised history. She wondered if she might have made a fortunate escape. This whole weird, one-sided conversation was leaving her wondering whether she should laugh or cry. Better yet, she felt a strong urge to throw something or just throw up. What could she possibly say?

A tap on the screen door preceded Stacy's impatient demand for Dieter to hurry. "You know Dad said we should be at the country club by three." She tapped her foot, and Dieter cast Bailey a sheepish look before making a hasty departure. Bailey turned back to the sinkful of dirty pans. With the now-cold dishwater dripping from her forearms, she watched the yellow sports car back out of the Morgans' driveway and race down the street with Stacy behind the wheel.

Bailey tried not to think. With exaggerated care, she finished washing the pans and straightened the kitchen. She was almost ready to check on her parents when she heard another tap on the back door. Seeing Gunter through the glass, she hesitated, unsure she wanted to talk to anyone in the Morgan family. Deciding he wasn't his brother, she opened the door and stepped outside. Without speaking, they made their way to the garden bench that had played a prominent role in the imaginary games of their childhood.

When both were seated, Gunter ran his fingers through his hair and seemed at a loss for words. Bailey said nothing. He was the one who had initiated this encounter or whatever it was. She wouldn't help him out. Finally he spoke.

"Bailey, I'm sorry—"

"Don't you dare apologize for your brother."

"I'm not apologizing for him. I'm apologizing for letting him get you alone. I'm apologizing for letting him hurt you again. I knew you'd be angry if he tried to feed you his amended version of what happened between you two, and I honestly tried to protect you from that."

Bailey's shoulders sagged. "Whatever was between us is over and done with. Why does he care what I think now?"

"I don't think you ever knew Dieter as well as you thought you did." Gunter stared off into the distance, seeing something she didn't. "He has always wanted to be liked and admired. He also dreamed of being wealthy and important. I think it's called a hero complex. You were the top athlete and scholar while we were growing up. You were recruited by some of the best schools both for your athletic and your scholastic abilities. In addition, you're beautiful. It fed his ego to be seen with you."

"Then he met Stacy." Bailey detected a hint of bitterness in her own words.

"Yes, he met Stacy. She's not only smart, athletic, and pretty, but her daddy has lots of money. And to answer your question, he cares what you think because he and his father-in-law have a political career all mapped out for him, and he doesn't want you to bad-mouth him and spoil his chances of being elected."

Bailey felt something cold and hard invade her chest. Once again Gunter was taking care of Bailey for his brother, making certain she wouldn't interfere with Dieter's plans. "What does it matter? In a little more than a week, I'll be back in Chicago." She jumped to her feet and almost ran to the back door.

Chapter Nine

SEVERAL DAYS PASSED WITHOUT BAILEY seeing either Dieter or Gunter. Chad continued to ignore her every effort to reach him. Bailey started each morning running laps on the high school track, where she could be relatively sure she wouldn't see Gunter. He'd always preferred running in the canyon. Most of the current track team and a number of people she recognized from the community, as well as a few strangers, ran at that early hour too. They were friendly and nodded or called out good morning to her but didn't pause to engage her in conversation. As she circled the track, she enjoyed the sensation of early-morning peace.

Alone in her head, she found the time to think. For long stretches, she pondered her unfortunate relationships with the two men she'd considered part of her future. She couldn't get over how much it hurt to think they'd both used her. Gunter's assessment of her place in Dieter's life wasn't any more flattering than Carla's stinging analysis of Chad's attention to her. Her thinking seemed sharper and clearer in the early-morning mountain air, and she vacillated between hurt and anger. Was she unlovable? Was she particularly naive and gullible? Should she give up on the dreams she'd harbored of becoming a loved wife and mother and be content with a career?

When her thoughts became too much, she shut them out. Instead she concentrated on each step landing squarely, on increasing her speed, on the exhilarating burn of her muscles, and on the sensation of flying. Each day, she recognized how much she'd missed running.

On the fifth morning, a familiar voice hailed her as she walked off the track to begin a few cool-down stretches before hurrying home to help her mother prepare breakfast and keep her dad company.

"I thought that was you." Her former coach approached her with a broad smile. "I hope you're here to apply for the opening on the athletic department staff."

Bailey laughed. "Sorry, no teaching certificate." She picked up the towel she'd left lying on top of her backpack.

"It wouldn't take long to get one if you enrolled right away over in Cedar City."

"I have a job." She wiped the perspiration from her face and neck. "I'm just visiting my family for a couple of weeks."

"I heard about your dad. Is he doing okay?"

"Yes. He's a hard man to keep down. His doctor wants him to take gradual steps getting back to his usual routine, but he's already fussing about getting the rest of his garden planted and finishing the pruning he was working on when he had the heart attack."

"That doesn't surprise me a bit." Coach Penter chuckled. "Dallas is a lot like his daughter. You never could accept a job half done or a goal unmet. Which reminds me, I'm really not kidding about wanting you to come work with me. I've no doubt you're doing an excellent job with that fancy big-city job of yours. You're probably making a lot more money than you'd get as an assistant coach at Hopewell High School too. You never did lack for smarts, but I've watched you run this past week, and I think your heart is still out there on the track. Remember, there's a time to follow your head and a time to follow your heart."

Twice she'd thought she was following her heart, and where had that gotten her? "I'll keep that in mind," she responded as cheerfully as she could. "I've got to go now. I don't want Mom worrying about me because I'm late getting back." She left her old friend and mentor, and as she drove her mother's car back to the house, she wished life's decisions were as easy as Coach Penter made them sound. She wasn't anxious to return to Chicago and hadn't decided whether she'd apply for Chad's old job. The job entailed long hours and a great deal of tedious attention to trends, data processing, and meticulous record keeping. She had friends in Chicago, but no one she'd miss a great deal if she never went back. Maybe *acquaintances* would be a more accurate term; her job kept her so busy she didn't really have time for friends, and if she joined the executives' ranks, it would get worse.

She loved the slower lifestyle of her hometown, but moving back in with her parents would make her feel like a failure. Of course, she could rent a house or apartment of her own as soon as she found a job. She was scheduled to leave in two days; she'd have to make some decisions soon.

She pulled into the driveway and noticed that the tree her father had been pruning when he'd had his heart attack looked neat and tidy, with no sign of the offending dead branch. Surely her father hadn't finished the job!

As soon as she entered the house, her mother met her with a happy smile. "Did you see what Gunter did? I was about to call the county offices to see who they'd recommend to remove that dead branch when I looked out the window and saw Gunter working on it. He cut it up for firewood too. I invited him to breakfast to thank him, but he said he had a meeting in St. George he'd be late for if he didn't leave right away."

A strange feeling, almost an ache, struck Bailey. Not until she was in the shower did she realize the feeling was disappointment. Shaking her wet hair out of her eyes, she pondered her odd reaction to hearing Gunter had gone to St. George. She'd been avoiding him all week, so it didn't make sense to regret that he wouldn't be sharing breakfast with her.

Chapter Ten

"I'm fine. You worry too much," her father said, protesting her offer to request another week's leave from her job. "I'm getting around pretty well, and you know the doctor said I should get some exercise."

"Mild exercise, Dad."

"Whatever. Anyway, Gunter is right next door if I need something I can't handle myself."

There it was. Another reference to how kind and helpful Gunter was. As long as she could remember, everyone had sung good old dependable Gunter's praises. Even she acknowledged he could always be counted on, just like she knew he would be ringing the doorbell in five minutes to take her back to Salt Lake to catch her flight to Chicago. She'd hoped Jamie would be able to make the trip to get her, but she was committed to assisting with Ashley's kindergarten field trip. Besides, being seven months pregnant, Jamie wasn't comfortable driving three hours each way.

Right on schedule, the doorbell rang, precipitating a flurry of farewell hugs and admonitions. Gunter picked up her suitcase and stowed it in the trunk of his car. Bailey waved to her parents from the passenger seat and watched through the car window until her parents and her childhood home were out of sight. Melancholy? Nostalgia? The feeling that settled like a lump in her throat had never been so strong before on taking leave of her family.

Turning to Gunter, she noticed his set jaw and recalled he'd been quieter than usual since his arrival at her parents' home, making no attempt to involve her in conversation. Her eyes roamed across his strong chin, took in his high cheekbones, and noted that his blond hair had turned brown. She wondered why she'd never noticed before that he was really a handsome man. Startled by her thoughts, she searched for something to talk about. Perhaps he could help her decide what to do about her job. She wouldn't mention Chad. He had no part in her decision now. "I'm kind of at a crossroads in my career right now," she began.

"I thought you loved your job." Gunter gave her a quick glance before returning his attention to the road.

"It's challenging, and there are parts I enjoy, but my boss just received a big promotion, and I need to decide if I want to apply for the post he left."

"I don't see the problem. It sounds like the big career advancement you've always dreamed about. You've always been up for a challenge. Don't you think you can handle it?"

"I don't doubt I can do the job. I've been doing most of it for almost a year already. I'm just not certain I want to. Dad's heart attack and being home the past couple of weeks have made me think of other things that matter to me. I'm not sure I want to be so far from family anymore." She didn't add that the generosity of her parents' neighbors these past two weeks and the warmth of their church members had reminded her of how much she was missing in her current work-centered life.

"Have you prayed about it?"

"I've been doing a lot of praying lately," she said. "I'm not getting answers."

"Sometimes answers don't come as quickly as we'd like."

She thought she detected a note of discouragement in his voice. It wasn't like Gunter to show any signs of discouragement. She glanced at his face and decided she must be mistaken.

"We're almost there." Gunter changed the subject. "Do you have time to stop for lunch before we go to the airport?"

"We better not. We're short on time, and I don't want to miss this flight. I can grab something after I go through security." A twinge of guilt or maybe disappointment struck her. It would have been good to have one last meal with Gunter before leaving, and she owed him big-time for all he'd done for her and her parents.

When he pulled into short-term parking, she reminded him he could just drop her off at the curb.

"I'll see you inside." He pulled into a parking space and retrieved her bag. Keeping it in one hand, he ushered her toward the terminal, then the moving sidewalk. He didn't say anything until they reached the end of the line of people waiting to go through security. "All set?" he asked.

"I'm fine." She reached for her bag. "I printed my boarding pass on Dad's computer this morning, and I don't have to check any luggage. I consolidated everything into one carry-on." She hesitated. "I guess this is good-bye. Thank you for being my chauffeur and for all the kindness you've shown my family."

"Good-bye." He only spoke the one word and seemed a little choked up as he turned away. He took one step, then turned back. One hand reached for the back of her head while the other encircled her waist, pulling her closer. His lips zeroed in on hers. At first his mouth was smooth and firm as it pressed against hers, then it softened as her lips parted, welcoming his. Surprise at her reaction turned to warmth, then sizzling heat. Delicious shivers raced down her spine as Gunter's hands traced the curvature of her spine and hers responded in kind. Fire like she'd never before experienced consumed her. As suddenly as the kiss began, it ended, and Gunter walked away.

Bailey stood motionless, too stunned to even call his name or recall that she was standing in a public place. It wasn't until someone asked her to move forward in the line that she remembered what she was doing.

Chapter Eleven

DURING A LONG, RESTLESS NIGHT back in Chicago, while she pondered and prayed to know whether she should apply for the position Chad had left open, it occurred to Bailey that Chad's behavior had been out of context for a man who had no qualms about using people to further his own ambition. She didn't understand why he'd risk alienating her or anyone else who would still be working at the main office. He was too smart for that. Somehow he knew she was no threat to him, not because of her ethics but because someone else had already been selected for the position. Obviously he had inside information concerning his replacement. And perhaps he assumed both Carla and she would be so angry they'd leave the company and find employment elsewhere. She felt a momentary pang at one more instance of his betrayal, then a sense of peace. In all honesty, she really didn't want the position. She'd continue on as assistant manager of the department, but if the new manager preferred to select his or her own assistant, she'd be okay. Her work was exemplary, and she'd have no trouble transferring to another department—at least for the summer. That would be long enough to accomplish what she had in mind.

Memories of Gunter's farewell kiss kept intruding upon her thoughts concerning her employment. One moment she found herself reliving the most exciting kiss of her life, and the next she was scolding herself for not stopping it. It was one more layer of confusion she didn't need. She gave herself a stern reprimand for allowing an innocent gesture between old friends to consume so much of her time. In spite of her best intentions, not only the kiss but every moment she'd shared with Gunter persisted in invading her mind.

Bailey was glad Chad had already cleared out his office and was gone when she arrived at work. She had no desire to see him again.

Subdued greetings met her as she made her way to her office. Carla responded to her greeting, but the redness of her eyes suggested all was not well. "Carla, thanks for the heads-up. If you don't already have plans, perhaps we could go to lunch . . . ?" Her voice trailed off, seeing the look of panic on Carla's face.

"They're waiting for you in your office," she whispered.

"Who?" Then she saw Mr. Davenport poke his head out of her doorway, casting a disapproving frown in her direction.

"Uh-oh," she muttered and returned the frown with a dazzling smile as she marched with a confident stride toward the open door. "Good morning, Mr. Smith, Mr. Davenport, and Ms. Everett." *Wow! Two of the top brass and the HR manager! There is seldom good news if the HR manager is involved. Are they going to fire me?* She shook their hands, then moved to her desk to set down her briefcase and stow her purse in its customary drawer. She straightened, attempting to conceal her nervousness as she faced her visitors.

"Ms. Morris," Mr. Smith cleared his throat. "As I'm sure you're aware, there have been a number of changes taking place in the company in the past two weeks. Mr. Overfield is taking over our southern division, leaving his position here in need of a new manager. Our partner's nephew, Eric Stewart, has been named to head the finance department when he returns from his European tour the first of September. Until then, Ms. Everett assures us you are capable of continuing the management of any day-to-day problems that may arise. Mr. Overfield has been advised to stand ready to offer you any advice and assistance you may need. When Stewart arrives, he will, of course, have the option of choosing his own assistant. If he has someone else in mind for the department's number-two position, Ms. Everett here will transfer you to her department. I trust this is all satisfactory with you." He offered her a benevolent smile as though he'd offered her some great privilege.

It took tremendous self-control and a reminder that she needed the job, at least through the summer, to refrain from voicing her hurt and anger. If her smile and acquiescence struck anyone as less than enthusiastic, so be it.

The trio called a hasty department meeting to announce her temporary status as department head. She opted not to move into Chad's empty office and announced there would not be any other assignment changes.

In the coming weeks, she found managing the department challenging but soon discovered it wasn't much different from the work she'd already been doing and that Carla handled much of what she'd assumed had been Chad's responsibilities. She was surprised to discover how well they worked together. They disagreed only over whether they should make Chad's new job more difficult, which Bailey had no interest in doing.

Determined to continue the regular runs she'd begun while in Utah, Bailey got up early to run on the streets near her apartment and made time on the weekends to go to a park to run. Some mornings, she ran the two miles to work, then showered and changed in the company's executive lounge and locker room before starting her workday.

She'd been back in Chicago almost a month when she set out on a longer run than usual only to be caught in a fierce rain storm several miles from her apartment. The rain beat down, leaving her drenched and cold. She wished she were back home, sitting at her mom's kitchen table with a mug of hot chocolate in her hands. She'd made more frequent calls to her parents the past month, which left her with mixed feelings. On one hand she wished she were there to help them through a difficult time, and on the other she wasn't certain she was ready to give up big-city life for small-town living again.

Muddy water splashed against her legs, and her hair stuck to her face and neck. She couldn't do anything about the weather, but it was past time she did something about her life. Only she could determine what she wanted. Staying with Smith, Finster & Davenport was not an option. As long as she stayed with the company, she would be subject to political game-playing. She wanted no part of that. Something was wrong when her paycheck was the best part of her job.

Looking back at her previous choices in a moment of clarity, she wondered if she'd used Dieter and Chad as much as they'd used her. She'd projected her dreams of having a family onto them instead of seeing them clearly and sharing their dreams of the future. She didn't want to be a politician's wife, and she didn't want to pursue professional success at the expense of ethics and honesty. Had she somehow thought getting married would solve all her problems? Or did she think marriage would magically change men she knew deep down lacked the qualities she most admired?

Stopping abruptly, she stared at herself in a plate-glass window without seeing the straggling hair plastered against her head or the dripping-wet T-shirt. Instead she saw the face of one man who did share her dreams and her values, a man who had never let her down, a man she'd loved all of her life. A passing car further drenched her with a deluge of brackish water, which she quickly dismissed. She knew who she wasn't and what she didn't want. Perhaps it was time to leave the past behind and look to the future. It was time to ask some pertinent questions. *Who am I? What do I want? What is really important? Who do I really want to be with for eternity?*

She returned to her apartment wet and cold but feeling stronger and having a greater determination to act rather than react. With her new insight, the summer passed surprisingly fast. She registered for a couple of classes at the university, got involved with a summer volleyball league, and attended church on a regular basis. As the time drew near for her temporary position with Smith, Finster & Davenport to end, she took stock of the preparations she'd made. No way would she accept a position in HR working with Ms. Everett, who wasn't one of Bailey's favorite people and definitely not someone she wished to work with on a daily basis.

Bailey would give up her apartment—it was overpriced anyway—and head back to Utah. The coaching position at her old high school hadn't been filled, and she'd received word from the head of the school board in response to her request that she could begin the job as a permanent substitute on the condition that she receive certification within the year. By using every penny she'd managed to save, she could make it until she finished the requirements for certification.

Monday morning, Bailey arrived at the office five minutes before the scheduled start of her work day.

Once again Carla met her with a nervous smile. "You're supposed to report to Ms. Everett's office immediately."

Bailey swallowed a groan. She'd hoped she could simply resign with a letter. She hadn't counted on a face-to-face meeting with the formidable HR director. As she took the elevator up to the human relations office, she felt like a school kid being sent to the principal's office. She scanned her memory for anything that might be considered a problem during the almost three months she'd been in charge of the finance department. She couldn't find anything beyond minor glitches. In fact, she could take credit for clearing up a glitch Chad had caused that could have potentially cost the company thousands of dollars.

"Go right in." Ms. Everett's secretary gave a negligent wave toward her boss's door.

Bailey took a bold step forward. She had no intention of going out looking hesitant and beaten.

"Come in." It was Mr. Finster who gestured for her to enter. He closed the door behind her while she took notice that the other two partners were also present. Mr. Smith frowned and glanced pointedly at his watch.

"Ms. Morris," Mr. Finster began at once. "We invited you to meet with us to inform you Eric Stewart will not be taking over financial responsibility for the company after all, as he has decided to enrich his education with another year abroad. Therefore, and after studying the matter with great care, we wish to offer the position to you on a permanent basis, with a salary commensurate with this position. There have been no complaints during the months you've served in a temporary capacity, and we have found firm evidence of your capability." He quoted the staggering salary that went with the job.

Stunned was too mild a word to describe her reaction. For just a moment, she considered accepting the offer. Then she thought of all the preparations she'd made and the new dreams that filled her thoughts. "I'm sorry, Mr. Finster, Mr. Smith. I'm honored by your offer, but I've already accepted another position and given up my apartment." She didn't mention her new job was that of a small-town assistant high school coach and that her salary would be a tiny fraction of the one just offered her. She'd be student teaching at first, both for the athletic department and in math classes.

"You could change those plans and rent another apartment." Ms. Everett appeared incredulous that Bailey was turning down the offer. Bailey too found it almost too hard to believe she was saying no, but the warmth filling her from head to toe assured her she'd made the right choice. Just knowing she'd received the offer was ego satisfaction enough.

Chapter Twelve

WHILE COMING DOWN THE ESCALATOR, Bailey scanned the baggage area as though searching for someone. Recognizing the foolish action, she gave herself a scolding. *Just because he met me here last time I flew in doesn't mean he'll be here today. He has more important things to do on a Monday afternoon than play chauffeur for me. Besides, I'm a big girl and can handle this myself.*

Her parents and sister were the only ones she'd told she was coming back to Utah to stay, but she didn't doubt her parents had shared the news with Gunter. Feeling faintly disappointed that she didn't see him, she claimed her luggage and made her way to the car rental area. She planned to buy a car as soon as possible, but she needed a means to travel to Jamie's house for a quick visit with her first nephew and to make the trip to Hopewell.

The baby was asleep when she arrived at her sister's house, and Bailey didn't stay long, though she was glad to see her sister and thrilled to hold the sleeping infant. She wanted to reach Hopewell before dark, so she didn't dare linger.

Time dragged as she drove, and she couldn't help remembering the last time she'd traveled this route. Time had flown as she and Gunter had talked. It was hard to believe she'd dreaded that trip and worried she and Gunter would have nothing to say to each other. She tried to shut thoughts of him out of her mind. He'd made no effort to contact her since she'd returned to Chicago. The good-bye kiss that had rocked her senses and set off months of self-analysis clearly hadn't meant to him what it had to her.

At last she arrived at her parents' home and greeted first her mom, then her dad with a hug.

"It's good to have you back." Her dad beamed as he released his hold on her. She was relieved to see he looked like his old self and had even gained back a few pounds. The yard looked neat and tidy, which made her worry that he was overdoing and risking another heart attack.

She tried to avoid looking at the house next door. Surely if Gunter was there, he'd come over to say hello. But he didn't come, and she took care not to ask her parents about him.

She awoke the next morning, anxious to put her plans into action. She couldn't resist a quick peek through her bedroom window at the house next door before donning an old pair of shorts and hurrying to the high school for her run. She didn't see Coach Penter but knew he'd be around soon enough. They'd talked on the phone several times over the past few weeks, and she wanted everything ready to begin working with him as Southern Utah University's student-teaching program outlined.

After her run, she took a quick shower, poured herself a bowl of cereal for a hasty breakfast, then followed her parents to St. George to turn in her rental car. That done, her father helped her find a used car to purchase. He seemed determined to check every lot in town but finally agreed on a small car that was clean and would get good gas mileage. They then stopped at the college, where Bailey filled out papers and paid fees.

"All right. That's done. Let's go to lunch," her mother proposed. Bailey suspected her mother was more concerned with finding an excuse to get her father to sit down and rest than with eating after their car-shopping adventure. They took their time with a leisurely lunch before starting back to Hopewell.

Once again Bailey found her eyes straying toward the Morgan home as she drove into her parents' driveway. Could Gunter be away? He said he sometimes had to travel. *Stop it!* she admonished herself. *You obviously read way too much into one kiss.*

Two weeks later, as Bailey prepared for her morning run, she realized she didn't miss her former job at all. Sometimes she missed having her own apartment, though she appreciated having a place to live rent free until she could find a place of her own, and she enjoyed her parents' company. Their differences were minor and involved matters Bailey considered trivial, such as when she wanted a granola bar and a chocolate-flavored vitamin drink for breakfast but her mom insisted on oatmeal, eggs, and sausage.

She liked her instructors at the college and loved working with Coach Penter. The math teacher she was supposed to work with was pregnant and missed so many days that Bailey felt like the classes were already hers. Most of the time she felt good about the choices she'd made, but she regretted waiting too long to recognize her feelings for Gunter.

Bailey stopped to fasten her shoes and make certain her phone was clipped to her shorts before starting her run. Since arriving back in her hometown, she'd run every morning on the high school track. In her mind, she associated her favorite canyon trail with Gunter and had avoided it, hoping the next time she ran the canyon trail, he'd run with her. Today, the trail seemed to call to her.

From the moment she turned from the pavement to the dirt trail leading into the box canyon, she felt the difference. She enjoyed running on a track, but the open trail was best of all. Air filled her lungs, the sun felt brighter, and cares seemed to slide away. Setting a steady pace, she followed the familiar route as it gradually led deeper into the narrow crack between the mountains.

Once she thought she saw movement ahead, but when she saw nothing more, she dismissed it as imagination. It wasn't unheard of for an occasional mountain lion or other wildlife to be seen in the canyon, but she'd never seen anything larger than a rock chuck and a few rabbits.

She was almost to the large rock where she and Gunter had often paused before starting their return trip. Her pace increased. The path curved, and there was the rock. A surge of disappointment swept over her. No familiar figure leaned against the rock, waiting for her. She hadn't realized how much she'd secretly hoped Gunter would be there, though her practical side had warned her she was harboring an unreasonable expectation. She'd been home two weeks and had seen no indication that he was still staying in his parents' home.

Slowly she approached the rock and seated herself where she'd sat so many times before beside Gunter. Melancholy chased away the bright September sunshine, and her heart felt heavy. *How could I be so blind? Why did I never really see Gunter?* She couldn't help wondering if she'd made a mistake in returning to Hopewell. Had he moved on just when she'd realized he was a necessary part of her life? Moisture gathered in her eyes, and she struggled to keep from sobbing out loud.

A whisper of sound caught her attention. She focused on the distant noise and heard the distinct sound of rapid footfalls slapping against the hard dirt trail. Someone was coming. She reached for a tissue to wipe her eyes before standing to begin her return journey. She had no desire to engage in polite conversation with another runner.

A man in shorts and a T-shirt emerged from the trees and loped toward her. Her heart suddenly beat double time. Gunter had come! She took a step toward him, and he seemed to freeze in place. She stopped too, and they stood half a dozen steps apart, staring at each other.

"Bailey?" He seemed surprised to see her. He hadn't come looking for her. He'd merely chosen to run in the canyon that morning and hadn't expected to find her there. Her heart took another roller-coaster dive, and a shiver of cold snaked its way through her.

Gunter found his voice first. "I didn't know you were back. Is everything okay? I've been out of town a lot lately and haven't talked to your parents for a month."

Warmth seeped back into her veins as she realized he hadn't been avoiding her. She offered a tentative smile. "I've come home to stay, and everything is fine now that you're here." Did she say too much? Something in her voice must have given away her true feelings. He took a step toward her, and unable to resist, she met him halfway.

His arms wrapped around her and drew her closer. His eyes looked into hers, searching. Evidently satisfied with what he saw, his lips met hers as though he would devour her, then gradually softened as she matched his fervor. Shivers raced up and down Bailey's spine as she leaned into him, and his fingers left trails of fire as they roamed her back. She couldn't get enough of him. Her lips explored his, and time evaporated like a wisp of smoke. Nothing had ever felt as right as being in Gunter's arms.

He was the first to pull back. He gave her a lopsided grin. "I feel like I just slew forty dragons to win the fair damsel."

"Just one thick cabbagehead." She grinned back.

"You never did let me win." Gunter pretended to pout. "From the moment I removed your shoes to free you from the clutches of that monster tree in your front yard when we were six, my heroic efforts have been for naught."

"Not entirely. Every knight in shining armor is bound to have an off day now and then. The important thing is even the most foolish damsel in distress—or cabbagehead, as the case may be— can count herself lucky to be rescued by a knight with magic kisses."

"Want to try that old magic again?" His grin widened, and his eyes sparkled.

She only nodded, suddenly feeling shy.

He pulled her closer, and his voice was an alluring whisper. "How about lunch today at that café next to Mr. Bronson's jewelry store?"

"And do you plan to do a little shopping?" she asked in a pseu-do-innocent voice.

"Whatever m' lady wants."

"This lady wants you."

"You've got me. In fact, you've had me for a long time. I'll thank God every day for the rest of my life that you decided to come back home. I love you and want to marry you. If you say yes, we can stop at Bronson's before lunch to choose a diamond to seal the deal." His hands spanned her waist, drawing her closer, and her arms wound around his back. Their lips met, leaving no doubt she'd come home to stay.

About the Author

Jennie Hansen graduated from Ricks College in Idaho, then Westminster in Utah. She has been a freelance magazine writer, newspaper reporter, editor, and librarian. She is the author of twenty-five novels and numerous short stories and articles.

She was born in Idaho Falls, Idaho, and has lived in Idaho, Montana, and Utah. She has received numerous writing awards from the Utah and National Federation of Press Women and received the first Whitney Lifetime Achievement award.

Jennie has been active in church and community affairs. She served a term on the Kearns Town Council, two terms on the Salt Palace Advisory Board, and was a delegate to the White House Conference on Libraries and Information Services. She currently serves at the Oquirrh Mountain Temple.

She and her husband live in Salt Lake County and are the parents of five children. When she's not reading or writing, she enjoys spending time with her grandchildren or gardening.

Three Little Words

Words

K.C. Grant

Thanks, Carrie, for the weekend research trip!

Chapter One

"YOU CAN DETERMINE A PERSON'S future by the first three words that come out of their mouth." As if to emphasize the truthfulness of the statement, Elizabeth Harding sat up straight in her chair, brushed some errant crumbs off her black pencil skirt with one hand and, while still flourishing a bagel in the other, added, "Prove me wrong!"

Her best friend and roommate, Andrea, let a small smirk lift the corner of her mouth. "I'm afraid to respond."

So instead they sat in silence, eating their breakfast until the middle-aged woman who'd been bussing the table next to them came over and asked in a heavy Bronx accent, "Cawfe awl right?"

Elizabeth gestured impatiently at her half-full glass of orange juice while her friend took another sip of her coffee and gave a smile. The server shrugged and left.

"See what I mean?" Elizabeth continued, her eyes rolling. "Besides, Andrea, you should know better than anybody that the way a person speaks can be the number-one factor that holds them back in life. You used to think Spanglish was an official language." Her friend squirmed a little in her seat. "But look at you now! Not that I'm trying to take full credit for your success."

"You never do," Andrea muttered under her breath.

Elizabeth took a sip of juice. "I'm not saying anything you don't already know. When you first came to Manhattan, you thought the big broadcasting networks would welcome you with open arms. But you soon realized all the stations wanted you for your ethnic looks . . . not your accent."

"I know! They wanted to make sure they had plenty of Latinas on their roster as long as they spoke like they were born and bred in the Midwest."

"Exactly. That's my point. When I met you five years ago, your biggest accomplishment was doing weekend traffic reports at the local station. But all that changed last year when I took you on as a client."

Andrea's eyes narrowed. "Your first *real* client, if I remember correctly. I'll admit that your ideas to help me rid myself of my Long Island accent worked. But helping someone move up in their job is a far cry from suggesting that you can determine a person's entire future by a few words they say. Your attitude isn't very different from all of those network producers I encountered."

"That's not fair," Elizabeth said. "I at least sympathize and understand that there's a double standard. My current clients accept that they are judged from the moment they open their mouths. But all that can be changed. Trust me. I spent two years studying this. In fact"—she tapped a finger against her chin—"I'd bet I could take anyone—say, someone in this very room—and I could convince their friends and family they'd suddenly been given an Ivy League education."

Andrea laughed. "That's hardly difficult here in the financial district. Half of the people in this room are probably interns for some high-powered attorney or Wall Street broker."

"Oh, not everyone," she said, glancing around the busy coffee shop with a sigh. "There's a handful practically *screaming* out for help. If only they knew where to turn."

* * *

As soon as Matthew Decker entered the coffee shop, he saw his friend Tyler waiting in line.

"Hey, man. Sorry I'm late."

"That's okay. I've been making my way through the usual morning rush. You look like you're still waiting to clean up after milking the cows. Do you really have to wear those boots all the time?"

Matt looked down. "They're comfortable. I'm a comfort guy. And I prefer them to wearing a noose around my neck like you."

"All right, truce. I'm glad you're settling in. I'll bet it's nice to have a couple days to kill before the weekend. Better than those overnighters before you rush off to who knows where for another assignment."

"I know." Matt ran a hand through his tousled blond hair. "Those were murder. At least it's not all business this time either."

"Does that mean you'll be looking for a little pleasure?" his friend asked.

"Let's not get carried away."

"You'll have to start wearing some of the suits you still have packed if you're going to attract any of these sophisticated women." As they made their way to the front of the line, an attractive redhead with curves in all the right places stumbled up against Matt.

"Oh, sorry," she said in a breathless gasp. "These heels weren't meant for running."

Matt looked down her slender legs to the three-inch stilettos she was wearing.

"You must be late for something if you're running," Tyler said, grinning.

"Oh, I could never be late enough to miss out on a conversation with two gorgeous gentlemen. My friends can wait." She quickly placed her order and then leaned back against the counter. "What do you fine young men have planned for such a beautiful summer day? Surely not boring old work?" She eyed them up and down.

"Unfortunately, I am due at the office in just a few," Tyler replied with an exaggerated sigh. "But my friend here barely hopped off a plane from Texas and is in need of some feminine companionship to show him around this fair city of ours."

"Oh my!" The girl squealed with delight. "Texas! Are you a cowboy? Maybe an oil baron? Oh, I just love a Texan accent—I feel all feminine and helpless when I hear that drawl."

"Well, go on Matt. Make her feel all feminine and helpless."

Matt growled under his breath. "You're gonna get it, Tyler." Facing the girl, he forced a smile. "Shucks, ma'am, I wouldn't know how to talk to such a purty girl like you. Why, I'm used to being around my cattle all day. They don't require much conversatin'. Yep, it's a lonely life. Why, there are times I dream about havin' someone by my side, someone who could help me roam the plains lookin' for lost heifers and cook my meals by the fire. Help me brand the cattle and hold 'em down when it's time for butcherin' and—"

"Uh," the girl interrupted, "that sounds really nice. You know, I think my friends are probably getting impatient. It was nice to meet you. Call me," she whispered, slipping a card into Tyler's hand before scurrying away.

"No wonder you don't have a girlfriend. Double decaf," Tyler said in answer to the barista's question about his order. Turning back, he continued. "Surely it must be lonely out there on the ranch."

"You really are gonna get it. All of us Texans *don't* live on ranches, and we *don't* all speak with a drawl."

"Yeah, and New Yorkers are all rude, and we're constantly getting mugged."

Matt grinned. "Touché."

Chapter Two

"Are you this brutal with all of your voice clients?" Andrea scowled. "Look!" She pointed, effectively ending the conversation. "It seems Melissa has arrived. Apparently she used the helpless damsel routine to cut in line."

Elizabeth raised her luscious cream cheese bagel to take another bite, then pursed her lips and changed her mind. The young men their roommate of six months had been talking to were attractive, especially the blond one, though he looked like he'd escaped from a rodeo. She'd never actually seen anyone wear cowboy boots before. Melissa probably had both of them asking her out before either one had ordered.

"Oh, I love living in Manhattan," Melissa said breathlessly as she joined them. "Excuse me, *the city*. I'm finally feeling at home. And if I meet any more successful, eligible men, I'm going to have to get my own personal secretary."

"So both of them were interested?" Andrea asked, winking at Elizabeth.

"Nah, just the dark-haired one. The tall blond one was yummy but not my type."

The server interrupted them again. "Heah's ya dry skinny decaf."

Melissa giggled. "I love ordering something that convinces me I won't gain any weight from it. Too bad they don't have skinny doughnuts or skinny french fries." She took a sip, and the cup left a frothy layer on her upper lip. She looked back toward the guys at the counter and licked it off.

"So what are their names, ages, weights, and bank account numbers?" Andrea joked.

"We didn't get that far . . . yet. Besides, I want to know what you two were arguing about at this beastly hour of the morning."

Elizabeth and Andrea looked at each other and shrugged. "Who was arguing?"

"Come on. I notice everything. That's why I'm so popular."

"Yeah," Andrea mumbled. "That's why."

"*Yes*," Elizabeth prompted, receiving Andrea's protruding tongue for her efforts.

"No, really, what did I miss?"

"Well, Elizabeth was bragging about how she could take anyone and teach them to speak like a walking, talking, blue-blooded American."

Melissa's eyebrows darted up above the cup raised to her lips. "Is that so? I love a challenge. I think we ought to take her up on it, don't you, *chica*?"

"Hey," Elizabeth protested, "I wasn't saying I really—"

"Oh, no," Andrea said. "You should be willing to back up those words. After all, we're talking about your future." She leaned in close to Melissa for a tête-a-tête. Elizabeth strained to hear what her roommates were saying, but to no avail. When Andrea sat up straight again, she had a smug look on her face. "All right, here's the deal. You're going to take someone in this room and turn them into a paragon of intellect and good breeding. And you've got three days to do it."

"Th-three days!" Elizabeth sputtered. "Some of my clients have been with me for three months!"

"Uh, uh, uh." Andrea wagged a finger at her. "I'm not finished. You remember I invited the two of you to the New York Press Club's journalism awards this Saturday? Well, that's going to be the proving ground for your theory. You'll bring your test subject with you, and we'll let some of New York City's elite determine if this person passes the test."

"Okay, fine. I don't think this will be as hard as you're making it out to be. I'll just have to choose someone—"

"Darling, quit interrupting," Melissa said. "It's not very proper. There are some conditions, the first of which is that *we*"— she gestured to herself and Andrea—"are the ones to decide who it will be. And, naturally, a bet isn't a bet if there isn't a little wagering going on. If you don't pass the test, then you finally have to come clubbing with us. If you do—"

"Proper or not, I'm interrupting," Elizabeth said. "If I win, the two of you come to church with me." Elizabeth ignored the look that passed between the other two. "I think you have yourselves a deal. Shake on it."

They did, and immediately Elizabeth's eyes darted around the room. *Who will they choose?* With her luck, it would be the waitress. She watched the frumpy woman clop around from one table to the next. It wouldn't be impossible to change her. Just improbable. "All right, so who will it be?" she asked.

Andrea and Melissa exchanged one more devious glance before Melissa smirked and pointed at one of the two men she'd been talking to in line. "Him!"

* * *

Matt and Tyler found an empty table and sat down.

"You know I was just messing with you," Tyler said.

"Yeah, well, there's nothing that bugs me more than when someone assumes they know you simply because of where you're from. Or how you dress or talk, for that matter. There are a lot of judgmental people out there, and I've had my share of it. And not just because of where I live."

Tyler took a sip of his drink. "Amen, brother! Look, don't take it so personally. We're all judged on first appearances. Take me, for example." He leaned back in his chair and puffed out his chest. "People usually assume I'm a rich, educated, and powerful broker when, in reality, I'm only a lowly intern. But I can handle it."

Matt laughed. "Sure, you've got it rough."

"It would help if you didn't dress like a field hand."

"Like I said, it's comfortable, and I clean up pretty nice. Wait until Saturday. Besides, why get dressed up to drink orange juice at eight o'clock in the morning?" Matt held up his glass.

"Coffee would look more sophisticated."

Matt shook his head. "You know I don't drink coffee."

"Whatever. It's your choice, man. But it's a lot easier to get a date with a girl if you look like you could afford to take her to Jean-Georges' instead of McDonald's. Of course, I could be wrong. I think our lovely assailant from earlier might have changed her mind about life in the big outdoors."

Matt jerked his head around to see three attractive women, all most likely in their mid- to late twenties, coming toward them. The red-haired girl led the group over, with a sophisticated Hispanic woman who looked strangely familiar close by her side. But Matt focused in on the girl with the white blouse and black skirt on the opposite side. Her dark auburn hair was drawn back in a loose bun, with a few tendrils escaping and brushing against her long, slender neck. She had a businesslike air about her, but there was a vulnerability in her hazel eyes.

They arrived at the table and stood right in front of him. The red-haired girl spoke first. "Hi. Remember me? My friend has a proposition for you."

Matt raised his eyebrows.

Her friend sighed. "Sorry. Melissa gets right to the point. It's not *that* kind of proposition. My name's Andrea Mateo."

"Aha!" Tyler said excitedly. "I thought I knew you. GMA's newest weekend morning anchor. So are you doing some investigative story? The struggle of the young, *single* urban man?" he said, nudging Matt.

"Not exactly," Andrea said. "And it's not *my* proposition." She turned to the silent member of her group.

The attractive girl stood dumbfounded, trying to compose herself. Matt wanted to touch her hand to calm her, but her ice-like composure returned, and she thrust a business card at him.

"I'm Elizabeth Harding, and I'd like to help you." While Matt struggled to ask what kind of help he needed, she surged onward. "I'm a voice coach or, more specifically, a corporate dialect coach. My friend told me a little bit about your . . . uh, well. You must be tired of being asked, 'Where are you from?' or having to repeat yourself to colleagues and clients. I can end that nuisance by teaching you to speak with a neutral American accent. You'll be more easily understood and will understand those around you more easily." She finished what was obviously a well-rehearsed script with a smug, confident look. "Uh," she stammered and looked around when he didn't respond. "I am willing to work with you free of charge for the next three days. I think when we're through, you'll be amazed at the new heights you can reach in either your career or personal life."

If Matt had had trouble forming a coherent thought before her speech, he was certainly at a loss now.

"Well, what a lucky day, my friend," Tyler said, jumping in to supposedly rescue him, though Matt was positive he had ulterior motives. "It looks as if fortune has smiled on us. Will you excuse us, ladies? To discuss your *proposition*?"

Tyler grabbed Matt from the table, and they walked a few paces away. "Oh boy. I had to get you out of there before you literally exploded. Can you believe that?"

Matt found his voice. "What did she mean by 'understand those around you more easily'? Where does she think I'm from, outer Mongolia? What a . . . a . . ."

Tyler silenced him with a glare. "Now, now. Let's not be thrown off by this. I still think this situation could reward us with certain *fringe* benefits. She may be offering her coaching service free of charge, but there's no reason it has to end there."

"Careful, Tyler."

"No, that's not what I meant. I wouldn't mind getting to know Melissa better. As for Andrea Mateo, hey, it doesn't hurt to expand your connections. Now, this Ms. Harding is another story. But so what if you let the ice princess coach you for a few days? You're leaving on assignment again after the weekend." He rubbed his hands together like an evil scientist plotting the end of the world. "Besides, what better revenge than to teach the teacher a lesson of her own?"

A subtle smile crossed Matt's lips. "Sometimes your looks don't deceive you. I think you're on to something. All right. Let's see how this plays out."

The two men turned returned to the table, and Matt held out his hand. "Ms. Hardin', I reckon you've got yerself a deal."

Chapter Three

ELIZABETH STRAIGHTENED UP IN HER office chair and tried to take a calming breath before responding to the potential client on the phone. "You see, my approach works quickly, teaching you how to form the sounds of the American accent even if you can't hear them at first. People customarily hear only the sounds in their own language until they're taught to make the sounds of a new accent. I've been retained by many notable companies, not to mention high-ranking politicians and broadcasting professionals. You won't be disappointed."

The party on the other line remained unconvinced. Elizabeth hung up the phone and slouched in her chair for a luxurious moment before popping upright to examine her day's calendar one more time. Mr. Giaducci was due in a few minutes: a decent enough man in his midfifties, trying to improve himself so he could run the family furniture chain and not have people think he was into stolen merchandise. Miss America Wannabe from New Jersey would come in after him. Elizabeth's afternoon was almost empty, but the lack of business wasn't the only thing causing her to tap her manicured fingers on the desk. *It's almost ten, and he still hasn't called to set up his appointment.*

The hours before Saturday were ticking away. Elizabeth knew her stress wasn't only because she was afraid she'd have to fulfill the losing end of the wager. It went much deeper than that. She'd worked too hard to get established in this otherwise unknown profession to have it discredited like this. She had to win.

Her cell phone began to chime, and she had to catch herself before she immediately answered. She took a breath, waited another second, then said, "Could you hold, please?" This gave her another moment to steady her nerves, not to mention it was a classic trick to give the impression that she was busier than she was. "Yes, this is Elizabeth Harding."

"Matt Decker, ma'am. We, well, met each other this mornin', and you made me a right interestin' offer."

"Yes, Mr. Decker, I remember you. I'm glad you called. You haven't changed your mind, have you?"

"Well, no . . ."

"Wonderful! Have you decided how you'd like to go about this? I do both phone call and in-person consultations at my office. I assume you had a chance to view my website and my credentials."

"Yes, ma'am, I did. It was mighty impressive. I never realized anythin' like what you did existed. I mean, I can see why the world is in need a yer skills."

Elizabeth really hoped he'd agree to coach in person. There was something about his tone that made her feel as if he was smirking at her on the other end of the phone. He wouldn't be able to hide insults face-to-face. "Well, thank you for the compliment. So . . . ?"

There was a slight pause. "In person, I reckon, would be best. If that's all right with you, ma'am?"

He was going to have to stop calling her ma'am. It made her feel like her mother. "Wonderful. Now, as for the location, my office is close—"

"Well, I was thinkin' about that, and I figured that since I'm only in town fer a few days, I'd like to see the sights as much as I can. So, if'n you don't mind, maybe you could do yer teachin' while you show this country boy somethin' of yer big city."

Elizabeth blinked. She supposed that would work. Usually she had a specific process for each new client, which consisted of video recordings and CDs and study worksheets. How would they do that traipsing around New York City?

"Are you there, ma'am?"

"Uh, yes, of course. I think that would be fine. I'll have to adapt my technique a bit, which might come across as unusual, but this is an unusual circumstance."

Elizabeth could swear he was mocking her when he replied, "You kin say that again."

* * *

Matt tossed his phone onto the couch, leaned back, and let out a hearty laugh. *This is gonna be the more fun than bronc bustin' on a bay stallion.* He'd spent the last hour researching cowboy slang. So far he'd made it through the *B*'s. He'd also visited Ms. Harding's website and tried to analyze the slick black-and-white picture of her on the home page, her eyes intently staring at him through the screen. There were links to pages of testimonials and vague references to the names of the many professional clients who had utilized her "unique approach" to stripping away the layers of the accents or voice anomalies holding them back in life. But the confidence of those words couldn't hide the fear he'd seen in her eyes at the restaurant. Matt had seen it in plenty of other instances. It didn't matter if it was fear of death or failure; the reaction was always the same.

Next he'd worked up an interesting itinerary, which would hopefully wrench Ms. Harding away from her starchily pressed shirt and pulled-back hair so she'd loosen up a little bit. It would be worth the effort when he came clean Saturday. He glanced at the clock. Since their first official meeting was over lunch, he'd better get ready.

* * *

The conversation Elizabeth had had with Mr. Decker had left her with the strangest feeling. She didn't have much time to dwell on it because the door to her office opened, and she was verbally assaulted with, "Yo, Ms. Hardin'. I'm heah. Justa minute."

Elizabeth cringed as Mr. Giaducci answered his cell phone and said, "Oh yeah? Whadya think I'm doin'? Wakin' my dwag?" Pause. "Nah. I've got this twakin' class I'm doin." Pause. "Whadaya gonna do aboudit?" A grunt. "Yeah, shua. Talk to youse later."

"Mr. Giaducci," she said. "Let's have you reenter and try that again."

The man rubbed a hand through his slightly greasy slicked-back hair. "Yeah, shua." He spun a 360. "Okay. So, how are *you* doin-*ga*. I'm doin-*ga* well, thank *you* very much."

Stifling her groan, Elizabeth smiled. "Better. And remember you don't have to emphasize the final *g* sound as much as you are. It's subtle."

"Sho thing."

"But you're making good progress . . . when you think about it. The trick will be to convert to the new dialect even when you aren't concentrating as hard. Shall we begin with our next lesson?"

She brought him into the back room where she had the audio-phone and speakers set up. "All right, continue with your vowels, and I'll play back your recordings when you're done. I'm sure you'll see that you've made significant progress."

"Shua, Ms. Hardin'. You know, I'm still gonna getcha ta go out to dinna wid me onuv dese days."

Elizabeth closed the door as a cacophony of "eeeee, aaaah, eeeeh, aaaah" sounds filled the air, and took a deep breath.

Chapter Four

"WELL, AIN'T THIS NICE," MATT said as they walked through the door at Katz's Deli. "I hope you don't mind, ma'am, but I had a hankerin' for some meat, and someone told me this was the place to come for lunch."

Elizabeth lived by the adage that the customer was always right, so she smiled. "It's a very popular place." Actually she'd never been here. It was one of those things tourists did, so she tried to avoid it. "You'll enjoy it," she finished lamely.

They took the ticket the cashier offered them, which Elizabeth assumed had something to do with the ordering process, then she watched the other patrons and figured out the routine: sandwich, fries, drink. Find the right worker and place your order. Matt hovered behind her as if waiting to follow her lead, so she confidently stepped up to the meat counter. "Well, let's see. I guess I will have a turkey—"

"Pardon me, ma'am." Matt tapped her on the shoulder. "I've been watchin', and those sandwiches are almost as big as Texas itself! I figured a little filly like yerself could in no way finish one off. So how about we share? Of course, I was really lookin' forward to that there New York pastrami I've heard so much about. You wouldn't mind, would ya?"

Elizabeth gulped. Andrea and Melissa were strict vegetarians; she couldn't remember the last time she'd looked at this much meat. "Sure." She let Matt step up to order the largest pastrami on rye she'd ever seen. With his cowboy getup, which included a Stetson this time, she was afraid they'd give him the whole slab.

They got their food, then Matt led the way to a table. She started to grab a chair but Matt dropped the food on the table and rushed to pull back her chair for her.

"Sorry, ma'am. I wasn't quick enough on the draw."

She shrugged awkwardly and helped him divide the food, taking a very small portion for herself.

"Why, that's not enough to keep a bird alive. Here, have some more fries." He dumped more than half on her plate.

Fries had always been her weakness, and she resolved to control herself. Delving into the matter at hand would help. "So, Mr. Decker, tell me a little about yourself. About your background and what your goals are in life."

Matt took a bite of his sandwich and squinted his blue eyes. "Well, ma'am, I was born and raised in Austin, Texas."

She paused to eat a fry. "That's a fairly large city, isn't it?"

"Well, sure is, ma'am. Right near a million. Of course, nuthin' compares to yer fine city."

Elizabeth continued to eat while she thought. Usually the stereotypical and traditional features of a dialect were stronger in rural areas. Even here most Manhattanites, especially her generation, were influenced by what was termed the "accentless American" speech found in the media. In the other boroughs, of course, it was a different story. But Mr. Decker's accent was strangely exaggerated for a city dweller, at least from what she could hear. It would help to record and analyze it. "I suppose your ranch is outside the actual metropolitan area?" she asked.

"Well, uh, that's generally where ranches are."

That could explain the deviations. "So you spend most of your time there? With your family, or do you live alone?"

He stared at her for a moment, making her blush. "Why, all alone, ma'am. It does git kinda lonely. Of course, I have my dog to keep me company. But it just ain't the same as conversin' with another human."

"Uh, sure." She thrust a couple more fries into her mouth and chewed before saying, "Let me tell you a little about what I've studied regarding your accent. Texan English contains a variety of different characteristics that are on no account universal, and each Texan may speak only some of these characteristics or even none. Just as there is no single Southern accent, there is no single Texan accent. The drawl of the Lower South has more influence in East Texas, while the twang of the Upper South left a greater imprint on West Texas. In South Texas, particularly, the Spanish and Mexican characteristics are heavily combined with that of the others—"

"Whoa there, ma'am. You've got my head spinnin' from all that high-falutin' talk."

"Sorry. Basically what I'm saying is that this is going to be a little more complex than I thought. Your way of speaking baffles me at times. And because of the time constraints, I can't break down your accent like I normally do and then help you work through each of the various sounds. We'll have to take a fast-break approach to it."

"Kind of like a stampede of wild horses?"

Elizabeth smiled. "An apt analogy. But if you're willing to try, I think we'll make good progress." She pulled out her briefcase and set several folders on the table. "I need you to go over these in your spare time today. They're recitation sheets. You need to do them in front of a mirror because I've given you some diagrams as well so you can check the oral posture of your mouth or, in other words, how loose or tight your throat and mouth are. Are your lips drawn back or puckered?"

"Puckered?" he said with a grin. "I might need to see an example of that."

Right then the owner of the establishment stopped by their table to ask how the food was.

"Why, you've done our Texas cattle proud." Matt responded. "I ain't tasted beef this fine since I left home."

The owner patted him heartily on the back and left them alone. Matt looked back at Elizabeth and smiled with those deep blue eyes of his. Elizabeth looked down at her plate to find she'd eaten all of the fries.

* * *

Matt insisted on paying the bill. "It's a gentleman's duty," he said. As he escorted Ms. Harding through the door, she turned around abruptly, almost knocking into him.

"Excuse me," she said, flustered. "Thank you for lunch. Let me know how those exercises go."

"You mean you're leavin' me here? I thought our time together was jist gettin' started." He purposefully leaned in closer. "What if I work on some of those exercises you were tellin' me about while we walk? Shorely it would help if you gave me some pointers, up close and personal. What do you say, ma'am?" He hoped he hadn't pushed it too far. He didn't want Ms. Harding to think he was some stalker.

"Uh, well . . ." She rubbed her forehead. "One of my appointments this afternoon did reschedule. Maybe I could stay a little longer."

For effect, Matt took her arm, and they headed left down Houston Street, which gave Matt an opportunity to play up his "ignorance" as he said in a loud, obnoxious voice, "Why, lookee there! I just noticed the name of that street. *Hew*-stun. Makes me feel homesick."

Elizabeth looked mortified. "It's pronounced '*How*-stun.'"

"Oh, well, there are some right interestin' names around here: Soho, TriBeCa, Hell's Kitchen, the Meatpacking District. Not to mention some place called Dumbo."

"They all have their names for a reason." She huffed. "*Soho* simply means, 'south of Houston.' And TriBeCa is an acronym for the triangle of city below Canal Street. And Dumbo is *not* a ride at Disneyland. It's the area under the Manhattan Bridge overpass."

She was a New Yorker, all right, with a typical "I can insult my city, but don't you dare" attitude. "Sorry, ma'am. I stand corrected. It sounds like you know your city pretty well. Have you lived in Manhattan long?"

"I opened my office here almost a year ago. My roommates and I rented a place west of City Hall Park, off of Warren Street. It takes the three of us to pay the rent. Andrea, as you heard the other day, is now a weekend anchor for *Good Morning America*, and Melissa is an aspiring actress/model. Whichever appeals to her that week. And, of course, you know what I do."

Yes, but I'm more anxious to know who *you are.* "Where did you live before that, ma'am?"

He saw her jaw visibly tighten. "Farther downtown. We'd better get to work on those exercises. Let's begin with your calling me 'ma'am.' I thought that was reserved for someone older than you."

"Sorry. In Texas it's kind of a catchall for anyone we don't really know well. Besides, I don't exactly know your age."

"Twenty-seven. And you?"

"Twenty-eight."

"See? Then we don't need to be that formal."

"So I can call you Elizabeth? Lizzie? Eliza?"

"Lizzie and Eliza only if you don't ever want to see that ranch of yours again."

Matt glanced at her out of the corner of his eye just to make sure she was joking.

Chapter Five

Elizabeth was starting to think Matt had some strange power. By the time they passed St. Patrick's Old Cathedral, he had them both calling each other by their "Christian names," as he put it. On the outskirts of Soho, she was talking about how difficult it was to run her own business. She figured by the time they made it to Washington Square Park, she'd be blabbing about how isolated she'd felt growing up as an only child. One moment she sensed she was part of a private joke, and the next he had her sucked into this world of gentlemanly behavior and Texas charm. He never failed to open the door for her, and he always made sure he was on the side nearest the busy road as they walked. He had a way of making her feel safe and relaxed, like she was sitting by a potbellied stove on a cold winter's day.

Great. Now she was even thinking like him.

Finally they made it to the park, and Elizabeth was determined to get back to business. They sat on a bench, and she began to explain to him the importance of vowel sounds. "The vowel chart I gave you is an extremely useful tool in learning dialects, including the neutral American accent, because it's a map that shows how parts of the mouth move to make the various vowel sounds."

"So it's all about the mouth, then?" Matt leaned in closer, making her feel a little uneasy.

"Uh, well, yes. You see, the vowel chart makes it possible to learn new sounds physically—"

A group of kids playing nearby lost their ball, and it rolled toward them. Matt reached down as one of the kids ran over.

The young boy grabbed the ball and looked down at Matt's feet. "Are you a cowboy, mister?"

Matt chuckled. "Why, I suppose I am. Should I prove it?"

The boy nodded his head, and Matt directed him to get his friend's jump rope. The girl protested at first but must have eventually been convinced it was important. When the boy ran it back to Matt, Elizabeth watched as Matt twisted a simple knot and then began to twirl the rope overhead, letting it fly so it fell effortlessly over a nearby fire hydrant. The boy cheered, and all of the children clustered around, each of them begging to be the "little doggie" as Matt roped them one by one.

Elizabeth couldn't help but smile. Then she found herself thinking thoughts she'd been capable of controlling. Until now. Quickly she stopped herself. *You don't have time for a relationship. Remember why you're doing this in the first place.*

Matt glanced back at her and then waved the children off with one hand. They groaned but returned to their play. He came and sat by her again and leaned back against the bench, his long legs stretched out in front of him. "Whew. I'm plumb tuckered out. Those young'uns got way more energy than me."

"They loved it. You were really good with them."

"I like kids. They're honest. They laugh when they want to laugh. Cry when they feel like cryin'. They haven't learned how to hide their feelin's yet."

Elizabeth looked pensive. "And they trust you. They haven't learned what real disappointment is." Another unpleasant thought. They were getting harder to shake off. "Do you come from a large family?"

"I suppose. Got me three older brothers and a younger sister. She actually reminds me of you."

"How?"

"She's very determined," was all he said. "What about you, ma'am—I mean, Elizabeth?"

"It's just me."

"No siblins a-tall?" She shook her head and tried to distract him with more instruction, but he wouldn't have it. "Woo-ee, I'm sure you got lots of attention."

"Sure. That's one way to look at it." She looked down at her watch. "I'd better be getting back to the office."

* * *

Matt plopped down on the couch in Tyler's apartment. What an afternoon!

He and Elizabeth had spent almost the entire three hours discussing the oral posture of the Texan accent: how he should avoid bunching his tongue against his teeth and instead focus on opening up the back of his throat. His lip corners were also apparently tense, and he needed to loosen them up, she'd said. She had some great exercises for that. It took all of his will power not to respond that he knew a few as well. Tyler was having way too much influence on him.

It was obvious he'd had a different goal the entire time: to loosen Ms. Harding up. There were a few moments that afternoon when he'd thought he'd actually seen her smile. But then she'd clamped up again like a bird's beak on a June bug. At least his sense of humor was pure Texan. He was having trouble keeping up the accent. A few times, he'd almost slipped and wondered if she would have caught on. She kept talking about getting him back to the office so she could record him, which was the last thing he wanted.

He was pretty sure the rope tricks had reinforced his cowboy persona. His granddad had taught him those with a bale of hay when he was a kid, and that was as close to roping a steer—or riding a horse, for that matter—as he'd ever come. Good thing no one but the cops rode horses around here, because he was a little afraid of them.

There was something very sad about the way she'd avoided speaking of her family. Again, he'd wanted to reach out and try to comfort her, but she was as prickly as . . .

Enough with the colloquialisms.

Tyler was supposed to be home around seven, at which point he would be getting ready for his hot date with Melissa. Matt would make himself scarce. He was tired of playing Bronco Bill. Opening the packet of information Elizabeth had given him, he stared at the vowel charts and exercise sheets. He was supposed to stand in front of a mirror and repeat a series of phrases over and over again. Fat chance. But he was doing everything he could not to outright lie to her, so he managed to pull himself up off the couch.

The only decent mirror was in the bathroom, so he went in and closed the door. Staring at his reflection, he pondered the same thing his family and all of his friends seemed to wonder on a daily basis: why was he still single? He was good-looking enough. Successful. He knew how to treat a girl with respect. Tyler would've said that was the problem, but it wasn't for the kind of girl Matt was looking for. The girl he wanted had to not settle for anything other than a strong, committed relationship. Attractive. It was best to admit that right from the beginning if he was going to dig deeper into what he wanted in a woman. He really liked long hair and soft eyes. Elizabeth had beautiful eyes. A slender figure was nice. Naturally he wanted someone who was intelligent and ambitious. He wasn't sure he wanted someone as focused as, say, Elizabeth Harding, but she was quite gutsy to have struck out on her own in such an unusual field. He redirected his thoughts. The girl had to be someone who had high standards. Elizabeth had rushed after a woman who'd left her purse on a park bench.

Come on, Matt. She's the last girl you should be looking at.
But he had to admit he'd been looking. Still, he didn't have much time, and he had a score to settle. Tonight. And he wouldn't take no for an answer.

Chapter Six

"The Empire State Building?" Elizabeth asked as she got out of the taxi. "So that's why you wanted to travel uptown. You're determined to turn me into a tourist, aren't you?"

"Yes, ma'am." Matt saluted her with a wink. "Let's go."

Elizabeth didn't know how he'd talked her into this, but she let Matt escort her into the lobby, with its art-deco murals and beautiful marble floors. Like most New Yorkers, she'd never considered visiting these tourist-bound destinations, like the Empire State Building or the Statue of Liberty, for that matter. With her luck, he'd take her there next. He seemed to know what he was doing. Somehow he already had VIP passes up to the eighty-sixth floor. As soon as they got to the elevator, they were whisked to the top, reminding her of the rides at Coney Island she'd loved as a kid. When they exited onto the main deck, it took a moment to steady her legs. Apparently ten o'clock at night was the time to visit. It wasn't horribly crowded; in fact, they found a secluded corner outdoors on the southeast side of the observation deck.

From up this high, she almost couldn't hear the traffic down below anymore. A brisk night breeze off the East River blew against her face. She closed her eyes and took a deep breath. When she opened them again, she found Matt staring at her. She wasn't sure she liked the look in his eyes.

"Even in the dark, the view's amazing," she said. "I never realized how much you could see."

"True enough. I ain't—excuse me. I have never seen anythin' so incredible." Matt whistled. "Look over there! Is that the Statue of Liberty all lit up?"

"I believe so."

"What a sight. I can't imagine all of those people comin' to this new country, none of them speakin' the same language. They got off the ships and didn't know where to go or what to do. But they all had that common dream to find somethin' better in life for themselves and their families. That was true courage."

"True," she said. "And yet most of them struggled for generations, mainly because of the way they spoke. It didn't matter if they were Polish or Irish, Russian or Jew; there was always somebody ready to judge them."

"Why do people do that? Why can't they wait to decide what someone's like?"

"I suppose it's a defense mechanism. We want to make sure someone's like us before we associate with them."

"So fear makes us keep our distance?" he asked, taking a step closer to her.

Elizabeth ran her hand over the length of the railing. "I suppose so." She moved away and started walking toward the opposite side.

Matt followed her. "Everythin' looks so small from up here."

"I guess everything looks different when you're up this high."

"True enough, Elizabeth. I reckon sometimes ya need ta look at things from a different perspective from time ta time. You realize that often places or even people are different than what ya thought."

Fearing this was a conversation disguised as a lecture, Elizabeth decided to stop it in its tracks. "Saturday night will be here before we know it."

Matt scrunched up his face. "Saturday night? I didn't know you'd need me Saturday *night*. I'm afraid I've already got plans."

Elizabeth felt a moment of panic. Why had she assumed he'd be available? But he had to come, or she'd lose the bet! "Are you sure? It's just that Andrea invited us to the New York Press Club awards banquet. I mean, this will be a fantastic event and a perfect opportunity to test out . . . well, to meet all of those influential people. There will be a lot of famous people there: George Stephanopolous, the mayor, the editor of the *New York Times*. Maybe your other plans could be altered."

Elizabeth felt like she was on the verge of tears. He had to come, or everything was ruined.

* * *

Matt couldn't believe it. This was going to be perfect. "Well, shucks, if it's that important to you, I think I could work somethin' out."

He could see her breathe a visible sigh of relief. "Thank you. I guess Andrea even has a limo coming to get her, so we'll probably be by around seven."

"Woo-eee, I ain't . . . I've never been in a limo before. Wait till I tell all the folks back home. They'll think I'm a movie star!"

He actually heard her mutter under her breath as she got into the elevator to go back down, "That would be the day."

As they left the building, Matt stepped out and hailed a taxi with a brisk whistle.

"You do that as well as any New Yorker," Elizabeth said.

"Well, how do you think we call our horses? Same thing."

She reached out her hand to him for a polite shake when a cab pulled up. "Uh, thank you."

Matt took her hand but didn't let go immediately. "I was thinkin' we could share the cab back. It would give us more time to . . . work." He knew that was the only way he'd get her to answer in the affirmative, which she did. But he had a different motive for the ride back. As the driver lurched away from the curb—which he knew was coming—he let himself fall against her. "I'm so sorry, ma'am. Didn't expect I'd be in the Indy 500."

"I'd apologize on behalf of all of the New York cabbies, but it probably wouldn't do any good," she replied. "At least they get you home alive."

There was an awkward silence then, which Matt was determined to turn into an awkward conversation. He looked out the window. "This shore is a beautiful city. All those lights twinklin' like stars. Of course, nuthin' can beat layin' out in the medder under *real* stars with your favorite gal. The sound of crickets beatin' out the rhythm of your hearts. It's a little piece of heaven."

"I'm sure it is." She shuffled around in her seat.

"Why, I'll bet there are any number of romantic places to go around here." She didn't bite. "You musta been to a few yerself."

"I suppose."

"Or at least there's probably places where your boyfriend takes ya that are plenty special."

She began to fidget again. "I don't exactly have a boyfriend . . . at the moment. I'm . . . between relationships."

"Oh." He was glad the dark hid his smile.

But then she surprised him by asking, "And what about you? Is there someone special back home?"

"Why, no, ma'am. I mean, Elizabeth. No one has my heart at the moment."

That pretty much ended their conversation until they reached her apartment. But the lesson wasn't over. He hurried and opened the door for her and escorted her to the front steps, where he started to lay it on thick. "I don't know when I've had a better day. It's too bad it has to be over. I wish it could go on and on . . . there's so much to see and do here."

"Well, I've been thinking about that. We're not going to make much progress unless we spend more time together. I mean, time working together. I'm prepared to take the entire day off tomorrow so we can focus on your lessons. If you'd like to come to the office around nine—"

"Well, I really wanted to see more of the sights."

"Then perhaps we can compromise," she said much too businesslike. "It's only fair that we spend part of the day in a more . . . traditional setting. If you have someplace you'd like to go in the morning, we can go. Then after, we can go to my office and work. After a break for lunch, we'll return . . . Well, you get the picture."

"That does sound fair. I reckon we can do it that way. You know, I do like a woman who knows her mind."

Matt had been purposefully moving closer to her as they spoke. Sure enough, she looked like a deer in the headlights. Now he reached out and grabbed her hand. For a moment, he could feel her pulse throbbing in her wrist. He held it tightly and heard her take in a sharp breath. Her eyes even closed halfway. Then he shook her hand briskly and said in a hearty voice, "Good night, Elizabeth. I look forward to tomorrow morning." He turned around and walked away in time to hide the smirk on his face.

Chapter Seven

"I'M GLAD TO SEE YOU wore your walkin' shoes," Matt said with a grin.

Elizabeth looked down at him from the steps of her apartment building. "Now you're making me nervous."

Matt watched her descend. She was still wearing her typical office attire, but he was glad she had on flats and that she'd added a cream-colored cardigan because it was a little brisk this morning. "Are you ready?" he asked.

She gave a weak grin. "Sure."

He held out a bag to her as they crossed the street. "I wasn't sure if you'd had time for breakfast, so I got what I was told were some of the best bagels in the city. Only I wasn't sure how you took your coffee."

Elizabeth smiled. "Yum, bagels sound good. But I don't drink coffee."

That was surprising. "I don't drink coffee either."

She raised an eyebrow. "Well, I guess the thing to do is . . ." She looked around and saw a homeless man sitting on a nearby bench. She walked over and handed the coffee bag to him. The bedraggled man smiled gratefully. "All right, what now?" she asked when she'd returned to Matt's side.

Matt wanted to reach out and brush back a lock of her hair that had escaped. Instead he gestured toward the park. They entered City Hall Park at Warren Street and ambled along the sidewalk.

As they crossed between the courthouse and the stately city hall, they saw several groups clustered on the front steps. When one of them parted, a couple appeared in wedding attire. A photographer snapped pictures as the two posed, and there were cheers from the onlookers, especially when the man dipped his bride and gave her an exultant kiss.

"They look right happy," Matt said.

"They should be, considering they haven't even been married a day. Give them ten years. Heck, give them one year."

"So you don't think it will last?" Matt frowned.

"Statistics speak for themselves. Over half of all marriages end in divorce. My parents didn't make it. But who knows, maybe they'll be the lucky ones."

She continued walking, so Matt gave a sad shrug and followed.

Elizabeth was the one to break their silence. "So, yesterday you said I was a lot like your sister. You didn't go into much detail, just that she was . . . determined."

"True. She's goin' to medical school in Houston—not *How-stun*," he added, for which he earned a laugh. "She's jist a first-year student, so she's got a fer piece to go."

"Don't forget about your vowel translation problem. You're transposing . . . sorry. You were talking about your sister. That's fantastic. Good for her for being so ambitious."

"The problem is, she was engaged when she started, and now she wants her feller . . . uh, fellow . . . to wait for her."

"And why not? School is important."

"Important enough to put off somethin' as valuable as true love?"

"If it's true love, it should be able to wait." Her pace quickened.

Matt matched her stride. "I'm not sayin' she's not doin' a good thing. But Adam loves her, and that's not somethin' to take lightly.

If I ever find the right gal, I don't think I'd let anythin' stand in the way."

Elizabeth didn't say another word until they exited the other side of the park. She turned and said slightly accusatorily. "What now? The only point of interest is to continue until we reach the . . ." She didn't finish.

"Shucks. You found me out. I thought it would be fascinatin' to walk across the Brooklyn Bridge. I heard there's one of the best views of the Manhattan skyline when you git to the other side."

Elizabeth frowned. "Uh, I think I might pass on that. It's a bit more of a walk than people realize, and I think it's time we went to my office. We really need you to focus on adding those final *G*'s."

He couldn't figure out what was going on. Why was she being so difficult all of a sudden? This wasn't the first classic landmark he'd taken her to. "Well, I'm sure it would be worth it—"

"No," she said, her jaw clenching.

He raised both hands in defeat. "Sure, let's go to the office."

Matt insisted on paying for the taxi, though with the traffic he'd rather have taken the subway. By the time they made it to the outskirts of TriBeCa, Elizabeth seemed to be her usual in-control self. After a few blocks and a right and left turn, they pulled up next to a three-story turn-of-the-century redbrick building. The driver stopped, Matt paid him, and then Matt followed Elizabeth up the short flight of stairs. They climbed more stairs to the second floor, and as she started to open the door at the end of the hall, someone interrupted her.

"Yo, Miss Hardin', I'm heah."

As Matt watched the pudgy, balding man stroll down the hallway, he heard Elizabeth groan. "Uh, Mr. Giaducci, didn't you get my message? I've cancelled all appointments today."

The man looked flustered. "Oh, no prob. I'll see youse Monday."

Elizabeth rubbed her forehead with one hand. "No, that's fine. We can work this out since you *are* here."

She ushered them in, and Matt took a quick look around the office. The room was light and airy, with cream-colored walls, twelve-foot-high beamed ceilings, and a large panel of windows to the left. There were two closed rooms to the right: the one with the large window in the door had to be the recording booth, and the other marked "Private" was probably her personal office. Otherwise there were just a few office chairs, a table, and a bunch of shelving stacked with CD cases and books on the opposite wall. A few tasteful paintings hung on the walls. A vase with fresh flowers and a couple of neatly arranged notebooks sat on the desk.

Elizabeth turned with clasped hands. "Go ahead and have a seat, Matt, Mr. Giaducci. I'll go freshen up. Uh, I won't be long."

* * *

Elizabeth went into her private office. A thousand thoughts buzzed through her head, the first of which was whether Matt liked her office. She'd felt like a schoolgirl waiting for her parents' approval as he'd stood there. That sensation was quickly followed by a sense of dread about what the two men would talk about when she left them alone. She definitely didn't want them to have too much time together.

She replaced her "sensible" shoes with an extra pair of black pumps, then retrieved a brush from the top drawer of her desk and pulled back some escaping locks of hair. A glance in the mirror revealed she needed a touch more of the power-red lipstick Melissa had suggested and a little blotting on her forehead, then she was ready to face them.

With a cleansing breath, she stood a moment at the closed door and then went to join them. "I'm sorry about that. I'm ready for you now, Mr. Giaducci."

"No prob. We was gettin' acquainted-like," he said. "You're a nice guy. Remember what I told you," he added.

Elizabeth smiled weakly as she led her client back to the audio room.

"Mr. Giaducci, what did you and my . . . friend talk about?"

"Oh, not to worry. I din't tell nunna yo secrets. I just told 'im that if you looked at me the same way youse looked at 'im, I wouldn't stand there actin' like I couldn't tell my backside from my front."

Great.

Matt was sitting on the couch, reading a magazine when she returned. "That should keep him busy for a while," she said. "And when he's done, we can start on a few recordings of your own."

"Shucks, then, let's get to work!" he said with what she felt was a forced enthusiasm.

* * *

After a few hours at the office, Matt told Elizabeth they needed a break. It wasn't easy stalling and pretending that he couldn't master the exercises she was giving him. And still she put on pressure to get him recorded. She told him he wasn't the first client who had privacy issues but that it really would help if she could examine his voice patterns more thoroughly. Finally he talked her into having hot dogs from a nearby street vendor, and they walked as far as the Hudson River. But apparently the sight of river barges and the New Jersey shore weren't that appealing to Elizabeth, who even said as much.

"Hope ya don't take offense, Elizabeth," Matt said. "I'm startin' to wonder if you even like this city."

Elizabeth turned to face him. "Why would you say that? I live and work here. It would be kind of silly to end up in a place I hate."

He held up his hands in mock defense. "Like I said, I didn't want you to take offense, but there don't seem to be much about this place that you enjoy. There are right beautiful parks, incredible restaurants, museums and art galleries, and the nightlife never stops. And there's so much more to New York City than Manhattan, but somehow I doubt you're interested in that either."

"Mr. Decker, you've known me for all of two days. How do you know what I am or am not interested in?"

Matt knew better than to kick a hive of bees. "Sorry, *ma'am*. My mistake."

Chapter Eight

ELIZABETH WALKED OVER TO HER closet, hung up her work clothes, and replaced them with a pair of jeans. Today had been a certifiable disaster. They'd barely been able to work a few more hours after lunch and not just because of Matt's lack of progress. She was starting to think she should back out of this bet altogether. Sure, Melissa and Andrea would love rubbing in that she'd lost—not to mention the price of joining them on one of their hedonistic weekend jaunts—but Matt couldn't seem to grasp the simple concepts she was teaching him, and her feelings about him were getting . . . complicated.

Somehow she heard Andrea's voice in her head. "Is that the real reason you want to back out?"

No. It was because today he'd managed to see right through her.

With a sigh, she went over to the window of her bedroom and looked out. She could catch a tiny glimpse of City Park from her window. Naturally Andrea had the larger room with two walls of windows that not only afforded her a gorgeous view of green trees and grass, but she could also see the top spire of the new One World Trade Center building. The people here in Manhattan were survivors. Maybe that was the reason she'd never really felt like she belonged. Well, one of the reasons.

She heard a commotion outside her door and went to see which of her roommates was on the move. It was Melissa. Or at least she thought it was her beneath the thick mud mask that made her look like an escapee from a B horror film.

Melissa looked at her in surprise. "Wow! I can't believe you're home, and it's four o'clock!"

"I guess I wanted to see how your half lived."

"Meow! Your claws are showing. Well, at least I have the excuse that I'm getting ready for a date."

"Sorry, that was uncalled for. I'm a little stressed."

"Naturally competition will do that to you. We'll try not to rub it in too hard when we win. Of course, from what I've been hearing, this might not be a total loss for you, so you're welcome."

"For what?"

"For introducing you to Mr. Texas. Tyler and I were talking last night and think you two are perfect for each other."

"Oh, you do?"

"Well, *I* think you're perfect for each other. Tyler's not so sure." She quickly added, "Not that I didn't defend you! He thinks you're not really ready to have a relationship with his good buddy. Maybe you're a little too businesslike, a little cold."

"Well, of all the nerve," Elizabeth said. "And I wasn't under the impression that I was supposed to have a *relationship* with Matt. I mean, we barely met, and I'm really only trying to help him, like I do all of my clients."

"So you don't really care about anything more?"

"Of course n—why should it matter to anyone else what I want?"

Melissa looked hurt. "Because after these past few months, I thought I was more than just your roommate. I know you haven't known me as long as Andrea, but I'd hoped I was getting to be your friend too." She stood and came over to Elizabeth. "To be honest, if Andrea was here, she'd be saying the same thing. I think it's time you decided if there's more to life than your business."

Elizabeth felt her chest tighten. "Right now there are few things more important than my business. I've worked too hard to get where I am. I'm independent now, and I can take care of myself. The last thing I need is a man in my life to complicate things."

"All right, if that's the way you feel. Hope you have a great evening." With a flounce, Melissa continued on toward the bathroom.

Elizabeth heard a ringtone coming from her room. She rushed back to her nightstand and grabbed her phone. "Hello?" she said a little forcefully.

"Ms. Hardin', ma'am? Sorry, but after today, I wasn't sure you'd still want me to call you Elizabeth. I'm sorry I'm not a better student."

"No, I'm the one who should be sorry. I didn't mean to be so impatient with you. I'm just, well, I'm under a lot of pressure right now, and I let it get to me."

"Which is probably a good reason why I shouldn't be takin' up too much more of your time. I mean, you've got real clients that need ya. I'm like a stray pup you've taken off the streets, and I feel right bad about that."

Elizabeth bit down on her bottom lip. "No, really. It's fine. I know we can do this. We have to hang in there. Maybe if you could practice what I gave you on your own tonight."

"Cross my heart, I will. And I've been thinking about tomorrow. I think we need to spend the day doin' somethin' not so stressful. Do you trust me?"

Trust. Not her strong suit, she knew. "I'll try." Elizabeth hung up the phone and then fell back onto her bed.

What are you getting yourself into?

* * *

"How was your date with Melissa?" Matt asked the next morning as Tyler stumbled into the kitchen.

Tyler shrugged. "Complicated. What about you and Miss Dialect Coach?"

Matt sighed. "Complicated."

"There's one solution, then, my friend, in a time like this. Let's eat."

They both busied themselves in the kitchen. Tyler started heating the coffee pot while Matt looked in the refrigerator for something other than restaurant leftovers and old brie. "We need to go shopping."

"I know."

Matt settled for some chow mein, which he ate with a spoon. "One of us should load the dishwasher too."

They fell into a comfortable silence as they ran through their morning routine. Then Matt blurted out, "I think I'm falling for her." He expected a gasp from his friend.

Instead Tyler sat down and ran a hand through his hair. "Me too."

"What are we going to do about it?"

"Not a clue," Tyler responded.

"So what did you do last night?"

"We went to the Met."

"You actually took her to the opera? Wow, should I rent the tux now or wait until it's official?" Matt said.

"Haha. It's not like I've met her parents or anything. Shoot, we've only been on two dates, though we do have plans for brunch this morning. She took me by surprise is all." Tyler took a sip of coffee. "Did you know she has a master's in business administration?"

"I did not."

"I think the acting and modeling thing is just because she thinks that's all a pretty face is supposed to do. But she's really smart. She could be anything she wants to be."

"With the right encouragement," Matt said with a grin.

"Exactly. Well, bro, I don't know what to tell you. After talking with Melissa, I think you might have your hands full with the Snow Queen. Of course, I've never complained about that before."

"Oh, git outta heah!" Matt replied in his best New York accent. Leaving his pitiful breakfast, he walked over to the window and put both hands behind his head. He stretched and took a deep breath. The city skyline was partially blocked by a nearby building, but he could still see the One World Trade Center as it towered above everything else—a testament to the resilience of human nature. No wonder New Yorkers were proud of it.

His mind wandered back to Elizabeth. This was getting way too complicated. He had to get out of it before he got in any deeper. That meant telling the truth. Soon.

Chapter Nine

"So where are we going?" Elizabeth asked as Matt held open the taxi door for her.

"Uh-uh. It's my secret for now. Remember? Trust me."

For a moment, she wanted to reconsider, but she got in, and they took off. Morning rush-hour traffic was horrific, as she'd expected, and several times she tried to engage Matt in exercises. He refused. "We're takin' a break. Even a hard-workin' cowboy needs a little time outta the saddle."

They arrived at their destination. After Matt helped her out of the taxi, he went around to the trunk to retrieve something. She frowned. "Central Park? Are we doing more walking?"

"Not exactly." He slammed the trunk and waved off the driver. "These are for you."

"You want me to put those on?" Elizabeth asked, staring down at the pair of Rollerblades.

"Well, not now. But you'll need them where we're goin', ma'am. Excuse me, *Elizabeth*. We had a deal, remember?"

For some reason, Matt seemed determined to keep her off balance. "I've never done this before. I'm not sure I can."

"Ah, shucks, it's probably easier than, well, fallin' off a horse!"

"That's what I'm afraid of." She groaned and followed him into the park.

"Call me crazy," Matt said. "I couldn't think of anythin' nicer to do on such a perfect mornin' than goin' skatin' in this here Central Park. It's the closest thing you've got to nature."

"That's true. I can't remember the last time I've been this far uptown. It is beautiful." She looked around at the verdant trees and grass-lined sidewalks, the bridges, and the ponds. You could almost forget you were in a city with two million other people.

Matt led her to a bench, and she sat down. Then Matt removed her shoes, replacing them with what Elizabeth knew Melissa would consider an abhorrence to fashion. She was beginning to think he was a little unbalanced himself. "So," she said, looking down at the top of his blond head. "How *are* the exercises going? You did find a little more time to practice, I hope?"

"As my grandpap used to say, 'You can always tell a Texan, but you can't tell him much.' I reckon that sums me up. Sorry if I disappointed you. I'll keep workin' on them."

"You might be surprised at how quickly it will all click in your brain. Remember, my technique is based on understanding the vowel chart. That makes it possible to learn new sounds physically, as opposed to relying on the ear, which may not be able to hear unfamiliar sounds. Your ability to hear the new sounds will improve as you—whoooaa!"

Matt pulled her up onto the blades, and she stumbled forward, falling against him. His sturdy arms wrapped around her, and she wanted to rest her head against his broad chest. His eyes met hers, and that was all it took for her stronger instincts to kick in. "Excuse me," she croaked, pushing herself away. "I'm not sure I'm going to be a good student here."

"That's all right, ma'am," he said softly. "It'll be nice to have us both larnin' somethin' together."

Elizabeth hadn't felt this unsteady on her feet in a long time— and she wasn't just referring to the blades. But it had also been a long time since she'd been able to breathe like this. The park really was amazing. As they skated by the pond mere feet from bustling Fifth Avenue, she already felt more peaceful.

* * *

Matt's fear that taking Elizabeth blading would turn out to be a big mistake was slowly dissipating. After two hours, both of them were still struggling with the finer aspects of the sport, but Matt was finally seeing that different side of Elizabeth he'd wanted to see. She wasn't just disciplined and principled; she was also bright and had a wicked sense of humor. And beneath that icy exterior, she was a very caring person. Having broken through part of that wall, he knew he couldn't keep up this charade any longer. Not with someone he was starting to care about.

But she was also very complicated, and he realized there was more to her wall than her dedication to her work.

They'd bladed at the south end of the park first. He'd let her play tour guide as they'd passed Wollman ice skating rink and the zoo and traveled down the well-known length of East Drive, under its cathedral-like canopy of elms. When they'd arrived at Literary Drive, she'd finally stopped spouting off about nasal tones and articulators and paused beneath the William Shakespeare statue.

"Good ole Bill Shakespeare," Matt said when he caught up to her. "*This above all: to thine own self be true.*" When Elizabeth's eyebrows went up in surprise, he said, "We do get a little larnin' in Texas, ya know."

She flushed. "That's not why I reacted. That's not what I thought. It's just that most men I've met don't really care for Shakespeare. Or literature in general."

"Then meet the exception." He bowed, throwing his balance off on his blades, and they both started laughing. Elizabeth reached out to steady him, then quickly withdrew. "So, Elizabeth," he said, trying to draw her back in, "which of the Bard's works are your favor-ites?"

She stood silent a moment, looking up at the statue. "What isn't to love? The stories he tells are about topics that are timeless: love, revenge, disappointment, greed, abandonment. It's the human story. I suppose if you're talking about his tragedies, it would have to be *Romeo and Juliet*. Of the comedies, *Much Ado about Nothing*. There are too many histories, not to mention all of his sonnets. Who can choose?"

"Well, I've got a favor-ite one of those." He began to recite, "Let me not to the marriage of true minds
Admit impediments. Love is not love
Which alters when it alteration finds,
Or bends with the remover to remove:
O no; it is an ever-fixed mark,
That looks on tempests, and is never shaken;
It is the star to every wandering bark,
Whose worth's unknown, although his height be taken.
Love's not Time's fool, though rosy lips and cheeks
Within his bending sickle's compass come;
Love alters not with his brief hours and weeks,
But bears it out even to the edge of doom.
If this be error and upon me proved,
I never writ, nor no man ever loved."

He looked over at Elizabeth and could swear he saw her wiping away a tear. "Did I say somethin' wrong?"

She moved away from him behind the statue and tried to respond nonchalantly, though Matt knew better. "That's a good one. In fact, you should quote Shakespeare more often—I think you started to lose your accent toward the end."

He clenched a fist, vacillating for a moment. "Uh, Elizabeth. There's something I should tell you." He fumbled his way to her side of the statue, but she was gone.

"I'll race you to the carousel!" she shouted back at him.

Matt sighed, but he always did love a good challenge, so he dashed after her.

Chapter Ten

WHEN THEY WERE FINISHED BLADING, they deposited their rentals back by the pond. As they exited onto busy west Fifty-Ninth Street, with all of its commotion and crowds, Elizabeth found some of the serenity she'd felt fleeing away. She sighed. "That was quite enjoyable. Thank you."

"You're welcome, ma—Elizabeth. This is a right peaceful place. I might have to set up ta campin' in the middle of the meadow if the crowds get to be too much."

Elizabeth laughed. "That probably wouldn't be conspicuous at all." She felt bad. He was probably homesick for the open spaces of Texas. All she'd known was buildings and noise growing up, and she imagined that too much silence might be as disturbing to her as the chaos and commotion were to him. She heard a familiar click that should have sounded completely out of place but really didn't and turned and saw one of the Central Park carriages coming toward them. She grabbed Matt by the arm. "Here comes something that should perk up your spirits."

Matt seemed reluctant to approach the horse at first, but she reassured him it would be all right. The owner was friendly and plucked at his bristly white moustache before motioning them forward.

"I'm afraid I'm 'bout due for a break, but I could take youse someplace if it's not fah."

Elizabeth smiled. "Certainly not as far as Staten Island."

"How'd you know wheah I wuz from?"

"It's a knack I have," she said. "Is it all right if my friend, uh, pets your horse?" She wasn't sure what the official term was. "He's from Texas, and he knows what he's doing."

"Showa, this one don't bite."

Matt was more timid than she thought he'd be, but he finally started to rub the white patch above the horse's nose and say something she couldn't hear. It was like that Robert Redford movie—maybe he was "whispering" to it. Eventually Elizabeth felt brave enough to reach out and stroke its bristly mane too. It felt like the hair of a girl she used to know who never used conditioner after shampooing. The horse let out a whinny, and Elizabeth jumped back.

She laughed nervously. "I think she wants you all to herself."

"Actually, *he* wuz twakin' ta me," the driver said with a chuckle. "It's time for his feed bag."

Elizabeth could feel the flush creep up her face as Matt joined in the laughter and said, "I guess y'all didn't understand his accent. Maybe you have some exercises for *him* to do."

"Perhaps," she replied, crossing her arms over her chest. "And I get the feeling *he* would be a faster learner."

Not to be left out of the conversation, the horse shook his head up and down.

"Look, let me give you folks a free ride crass the pahk, no chahge."

That gave Elizabeth an idea. "What if my friend drove? Or is that against union rules? He's a gen-u-ine Texas cowboy," she mimicked, "and I know he misses his horses."

The man scrunched up his face a moment before answering. "I doubt anyone'd mind."

He held out the reins to Matt, and Elizabeth climbed onto the other side. Again Matt hesitated, but then he obliged, climbing into the driver's seat. He took the reins and clicked the horse into action, and they started with a jolt across Central Park South.

They moved along the bustling interchange that led to Columbus Circle. Red tour buses towered over them, and they waved obligingly at the gawking tourists who passed by. Yet compared to the frantic pace of the city, the gentle trotting of the horse was somehow rhythmically soothing. And with Matt at her side, her feeling of peace returned, and she could have ridden around the entire park.

Matt, however, appeared to have different plans after they rode up Central Park West. "I think you'd better get your friend his reward for a hard day's work," he told the driver. "And we're probably due a treat as well."

She grinned and waved good-bye to the driver. "So what about that treat you just promised?" Elizabeth turned to Matt.

"Well . . ." He looked around, and she saw his eyes land on an ice cream cart. Then he bowed. "Your wish is my command, my fair lady."

He stuck with a plain vanilla cone, and Elizabeth opted for rocky road.

She moaned as she took a first lick. "I can't remember the last time I indulged in ice cream."

"You should do it more often. Life isn't only about work—gotta throw in a little fun too."

"I'm starting to believe you. This was the most fun I've had in a long time. Thank you."

The look in Matt's eyes made her nervous again. "I guess it's not how the day begins but how it ends that's most important," he said.

"Is that something your grandpap would say?" She looked up at him and felt her heart skip a beat.

"He was a great man. I've given heed to many things he's said." He took a step closer.

"What other words of wisdom did he give you?" For some reason, Elizabeth leaned toward him.

Matt reached out and touched her cheek. "To never let go of the things that are most important."

* * *

His hand stroked the back of her neck as he pulled her to him. Their lips met, and the chaos and noise of the city around them disappeared. Her lips were cold from the ice cream, but they quickly warmed. Too soon they parted, and Matt wanted to get lost in her hopeful eyes, but the guilt was welling up in his throat like glue. He struggled to speak. "Uh, Elizabeth. I know that we're ridin' with Andrea and Melissa tonight, but then maybe we can find a few minutes alone to . . . talk."

"About what?"

"Well, this is really hard for me to say. I know these past few days have been crazy and we've been spendin' a lot of time together. I want you to be clear on my intentions." He cleared his throat. "This isn't the way I thought things would go at all, so I don't know what to do. It's just that, well, I—" he stammered.

She reached out and touched his arm. "It's been crazy for me too. But you don't have to be afraid to tell me what you're feeling. Of course, you don't have to tell me anything you don't want to." She paused to take a deep breath. "What I'm trying to say is we can both take our time and talk when we're ready." She smiled broadly. "Speaking of ready, should we face it and go to the office?"

Matt wasn't sure he was ready to face anything right now. He was looking at her so intently that he almost didn't see the skateboarder hurtling toward them. "Look out!" Matt shouted, pushing her out of the way in time. He threw up his hands in defense, and both men toppled to the ground. Matt let out a grunt and then shouted out at the quickly retreating offender, "Hey, man, watch where you're going next time! You could have hurt someone."

He quickly looked back at Elizabeth and found her staring wide-eyed at him. "Are you all right?" He gently lifted her from the ground. "You're not hurt are you?" He pointed at the mess on the ground. "I'm afraid your indulgence has seen better days."

But she didn't seem to care about the ruined ice cream. "I think you just lost your accent!" she said.

"What? Well, I . . . I think you're right." *Now what, idiot?*

She shook her head in disbelief. "I don't know how to explain it! The only thing I can think is that maybe the adrenaline rush caused a shift in some of your brain patterns, and everything you've been studying finally connected. This could be a major breakthrough in the field of language study!"

Matt gave a weak laugh. "Maybe. I don't know how to explain it myself. Of course, forgive me if I revert back to y'all every now and again."

"Of course. But we have to take advantage of this incredible leap." Elizabeth glanced down at her watch. "Let's go back to the office and record you speaking again. It's barely one o'clock. We'll have plenty of time before we have to get ready for tonight."

"Uh, I don't know. I mean, obviously something's changed. So let's not tempt fate; let's try and accept things the way they are."

Just tell her.

But now didn't seem to be the right time. She was so excited. If he told her, it would make her look like a fool. Perhaps before dinner started he'd take her aside and let her know the truth. At which point she'd probably get angry and tell him she never wanted to see him again. Maybe before the awards. He'd have to tell her before then.

"Oh no. You're hurt," Elizabeth said.

He looked down and noticed a gash on his arm for the first time. "It's fine."

"No, you need to take care of that. We'd better get you home. The office can wait."

Their taxi ride was the longest of his life. Elizabeth kept a tissue pressed against his wound the entire time and insisted that he be dropped off first. As the taxi started to drive away, she leaned out the window and, with a hopeful smile, said, "I'll see you tonight!"

He waved back with a forced smile. *What have I done?*

* * *

"So what's up?" Andrea asked from the couch when Elizabeth walked into the apartment. "I know, I know. I'll try that again. Hello, how has your day been?"

Elizabeth waved a hand. "Right now, even bad grammar can't ruin my day."

Andrea's eyes widened. "Do my ears deceive me? That's like Melissa ignoring a run in her nylons. Seriously, what's happening?"

Elizabeth shrugged and went over to the fridge for a drink.

"Aha! I saw the expression on your face!" Andrea said. "You know the last three days must have been incredible for you to have fallen so fast. Are you sure? According to Melissa, you were still digging in your heels."

Elizabeth bit her lip. "I don't know. I want so badly for my business to succeed, and this could be a distraction I don't need right now."

"I know your independence is important to you. But is that the only reason you'd let him get away?"

Elizabeth didn't respond right away. "What if he thinks differently of me? After all, I judged him for where he was from. He might not think that I'm as . . ."

"Smart, funny, sophisticated?" Andrea filled in. "If he doesn't see that, I can always have a talk with him."

"Oh, no you don't!" Elizabeth shot back. "I don't know what to do. There are times when I feel so comfortable with Matt— like part of me has known him forever. I know that sounds cliché, but it's true. And yet, at the same time, I get the feeling there's more to him than he's letting me see."

"So which part have you fallen for?"

She looked up. "Both, I suppose. He makes me comfortable and uneasy. I never know what's going to happen next, but I can't wait to find out. But if he's everything that I think he is . . . can I risk losing him?"

Andrea began to applaud. "Bravo. And this coming from the girl who Googles the weather every single day because she doesn't like surprises." She stood and walked over to Elizabeth, placing a hand on her shoulder. "I'll give you the same advice you once gave me: something about having enough faith that things will work out the way they're supposed to."

"I guess I *should* take my own advice."

Andrea shrugged. "Whatever happens, this is a good sign. You're opening up. You've realized love may be more necessary than you think."

The tears in Elizabeth's eyes made everything blur. "I don't even care about the bet anymore. I'd rather have a chance with Matt."

"Good, because we're probably going to win." Andrea smirked.

Elizabeth gave a confident smile. "Don't be so sure."

* * *

Matt adjusted his tie one more time as he looked in the mirror. He'd wanted to talk to Tyler and get his opinion about how to get out of this mess, but Tyler wasn't home. This was no longer a game to Matt. The last thing he wanted to see was Elizabeth get hurt. He took out his freshly pressed tuxedo and laid it on the bed. He'd bought it to wear to his sister's wedding. At least he was putting it to good use. His phone sounded, indicating he had a new text message.

It was work—the only thing he should have been thinking about but the one thing that had somehow become his last priority.

The door to the apartment slammed. Relieved that he had someone to work through all of this with, Matt finished fastening his cuff links and went into the living room. "Hey, man, I really could use some advice right now. I think I got myself into a mess with Elizabeth. I'm really starting to care for her, and I don't know—"

"I'd hold that thought, my friend. Guess what I just found out."

Chapter Eleven

ELIZABETH LOOKED AT HERSELF IN the mirror. Her dark-emerald cocktail dress made her eyes look even greener. Andrea had loaned her a pair of diamond earrings and a diamond solitaire necklace, which sparkled in the mirror. She'd curled her hair but kept it long because Matt once told her he liked to see it that way.

Matt.

She was so sure he'd been trying to tell her he really cared for her earlier. But as she looked at her reflection, some of her fears came back. Maybe it was her imagination. To a lot of guys, a kiss was just a kiss. She'd hoped to talk it over some more with Andrea earlier, just to make sure she wasn't reading too much into it, but Melissa had chosen that moment to come flouncing in. Elizabeth had wanted to make amends after yesterday's disagreement, but Melissa had given her an icy glare and begun noisily preparing her green drink in the kitchen blender. She and Andrea had exchanged a shrug, and Elizabeth had left to get ready.

Was she ready to take this next step though? Could she really put her job and the past behind her and include Matt in her life? She'd fought for so long and worked so hard to be the independent woman she was today. This could change everything.

Ready to exercise that faith you've been preaching about?

The limo pulled up in front of their apartment promptly at seven. Elizabeth didn't know what the protocol was when the woman picked up the man, but they picked up Andrea's date before they arrived at Matt and Tyler's, so she gathered some pointers. She sat nervously in the backseat, fingering the beautiful yellow roses Matt had sent a few hours before. There had been a handwritten note attached, in which he had repeated that he was looking forward to this evening. But he'd added that she was stronger than she thought and could handle anything life threw at her. It wasn't the most romantic declaration, but the flowers were lovely, and she hadn't missed the Texas implication. The front door of the building opened, and Matt and Tyler strode down the stairs.

Her breath caught in her throat. Matt looked incredible in his tuxedo, but she had to laugh when she saw that he was still wearing boots. At least he was being true to himself.

Melissa excitedly threw open the door. "Well, well, look what we lassoed ourselves tonight. Welcome, gentlemen." She giggled and gave Tyler a generous kiss when he sat next to her in the rear-facing seat.

Matt took his place at Elizabeth's side. "You got the flowers, I see."

"Yes, they're beautiful. Thank you." She felt a little awkward but leaned over and gave him a quick peck on the cheek. She wished she were as good at reading him as he was at deciphering her emotions. He didn't seem to mind, but they didn't touch again the remainder of the ride.

With the six of them, there was plenty of conversation, and it made the limo ride uptown bearable. When they arrived at the Manhattan Yacht Club, a valet opened the door for them. There was already a sizable crowd entering the facility, and Elizabeth saw the bulk of the camera flashes coming from George Stephanopolous's direction as he shook hands with the mayor. A few lights gravitated toward them—after all, Andrea was something of a celebrity—then faded as they all made their way inside.

Andrea handed the attendant her invitation, confirming the additional attendees, and Elizabeth could swear she saw Matt and Tyler exchange a look.

"They got my message, so we're all set," Andrea said with a sigh of relief. "Our table is number seventeen. We're probably toward the back."

Melissa put an arm around her. "For now! Next year we'll be up with the VIPs."

A server immediately approached them with a tray of champagne. Elizabeth didn't take one and was surprised when Matt didn't either. There was a bottle of Perrier at their table anyway when they sat down.

The commotion was a little overwhelming: a hundred different conversations going on at once. They all appeared to be trying to get their bearings, with Andrea greeting one of her colleagues with a kiss and Melissa more intent on being seen. After a few exaggerated waves to people she probably didn't even know, she turned to Elizabeth. "You'd better start making the rounds. You know, to *test* the waters, as it were."

Elizabeth wanted to stick her tongue out but refrained from the juvenile behavior. She leaned toward Matt. "Would you like to socialize? Not that I know any of the more famous people here, but maybe we'll just bump into one of them and get an introduction."

Matt shifted around in his seat. "Well, I don't know. I was hopin' you and I could just sit here and talk."

"I know you're worried about fitting in, but you'll do fine," she said. "Your accent is hardly noticeable—just a few of those dropped *G*s—and you seem so much more confident. You'll be sure to win them over." She grabbed him by the arm and stood.

* * *

Matt stumbled as Elizabeth led them into the crowd. "No, really, I—"

They bumped up against an attractive couple. The man was obviously some high-powered *something*, and Matt wasn't going to guess if his blond companion was his daughter or his wife. They introduced themselves, but it didn't translate into conversation. At least he didn't know them. After the next couple made a tactful escape, Matt whispered, "I don't know. Most of these people aren't my type."

"Well, not everyone is as . . . formidable as that couple was. What about . . ." Her head darted to and fro as she looked around the room for a new target while Matt struggled to come up with an excuse to get her alone . . . *and* stay unnoticed in the crowd. As he looked for his own means of escape, his eyes locked with someone else's, and he knew the moment of reckoning was at hand. As the tall brunette woman came toward them, he realized he hadn't been this nervous since he'd stared down the barrel of an AK-47.

"Why, Matt, whatever—"

"Sandra, it's good to see you," Matt jumped in.

"You two know each other?" Elizabeth asked. "What a . . . coincidence."

"It sure is," Matt said. "It's good to see you. Uh . . . it looks like they might be starting."

The woman winked. "Don't be in such a hurry. They want to make sure we're all sloshed before they start giving out awards. It slows down the losers' reaction time."

Matt wanted to climb into a foxhole as Elizabeth asked, "So where do you two know each other from?"

"Work," Matt blurted out. "Uh, Sandra, this is Elizabeth. Elizabeth, Sandra."

Elizabeth's face scrunched up. "You know Matt from Texas?"

"Texas? No, it was Washington—"

"Uh, you know, it was nice seeing you, Sandra," Matt said. Elizabeth probably thought he was extremely rude as he pulled her away, but he was past caring at this point. He needed to talk to her. *Now.* "Elizabeth, can we go somewhere and talk? A minute is all it will take."

The emcee decided everyone had had enough to drink. "Welcome, ladies and gentlemen, to the ninth annual New York Press Awards dinner. Please be seated, as we'll be serving dinner shortly."

Matt didn't hear a word the man said after that. He numbly walked back to their table and pulled out Elizabeth's chair for her, then he sat down. He could feel the sweat on his brow as he poured a glass of water. Over the rim of his glass, he could see Elizabeth's confusion. Maybe she thought he was a player and would tell him to stay away the first chance she got. That might be better than what she was about to find out.

Chapter Twelve

THE FOOD WAS A CULINARY masterpiece, but Elizabeth could hardly taste it. From the melted brie appetizers to the filet mignon with gorgonzola cream sauce, she chewed and swallowed but felt it stick in her throat. Why was Matt so eager to avoid that girl? Her rational side kept arguing that naturally Matt knew other women and probably dated, and, well, it all made her feel like an idiot. So what if he had a past; she could still have a place in his future.

But he was acting so strangely. Even when they'd picked him up, he'd seemed distant and distracted. She looked over at him and gave a feeble smile, which he returned with a still-reserved look in his eyes.

Elizabeth took another bite of her chocolate mousse, and Melissa excused herself. At least now Elizabeth could resolve one issue hanging over her. She excused herself as well and followed after her roommate, catching her in the restroom, touching up her lipstick. "Can we talk?" Elizabeth asked.

"Sure."

"I'm really sorry about yesterday. I said things I didn't mean and let my frustrations get the better of me. Friends?" she asked, holding out her arms.

Melissa cringed. "After what I'm about to tell you, you might not want to be friends."

"Why?"

"This morning, Tyler and I had brunch at Poco's in the East Village. I guess I had a few too many bloody marys and got a little tipsy and let it slip that . . ."

"What did you say?" Elizabeth prompted.

"I might have let it slip about our bet." She saw Elizabeth's reaction and pled her case. "I thought you didn't care about him!"

Elizabeth clenched her fists. "Oh, sure, after all, how could I possibly care about anyone? I mean, all I care about is my business and how successful I am." She took a deep breath to calm herself.

"I'm really sorry. But that's pretty much the impression you tend to give at times."

Elizabeth's shoulders sank. "You're right. I'll take some of the blame. But things have changed since then. Oh!" She slapped her head with a hand. "What must he think of me now? No wonder he's been acting this way. What can I do?"

"I'll tell Tyler I was wrong, and he'll talk to Matt."

"No, I've got to clear this up myself. Maybe . . ." They heard the announcer begin. "We'd better get back so we don't miss Andrea's award. I'll try to talk to him after. We'll clear things up. Don't worry."

Elizabeth hugged Melissa, and they returned to their table.

Andrea's category of political coverage for the recent presidential campaign came up next, and when the emcee read her name, the three women reached across the table and held hands. She was up against some stiff competition.

"And the award for political coverage, television," the presenter began, "goes to . . . Andrea Mateo, formerly of Pix11 News!"

Their table erupted in cheers.

Elizabeth jumped up from the table and clapped with everyone else. It was so exciting to watch her friend scurry between tables to accept her award. Everyone sat, and Elizabeth reached over and squeezed Matt's hand. He was smiling, but she still sensed some sadness in his eyes. Needless to say, it put a slight damper on her excitement.

Andrea gave a humble acceptance speech, thanking colleagues for their support and her former employer for this opportunity. As she wrapped things up, she looked back at their table and added, "Lastly, I wouldn't be here if it wasn't for someone who had the courage a few years ago to tell me the one thing I didn't want to hear. *Gracias, chica.* And I'm glad you won as well."

Elizabeth felt her stomach clench. She was afraid to look at Matt. Andrea came back to the table, radiant, and held out her award for all to see. They echoed their congratulations and then contained their excitement as the night continued. A quick glance at the program made Elizabeth worry that the night was going to last forever. It was amazing how many areas there were in media coverage, from Internet to print to television to radio broadcast. Another half hour of awards passed, and still Matt had barely looked at her. She'd never get to talk to him and clear things up.

"And now the award for spot news," the emcee continued. "This is a special award given for breaking news that requires an immediate response. We had a variety of subjects this year: from hurricanes to wars and tragedies to triumphs. And the nominees are . . ."

Elizabeth had been only half listening until she heard, "And lastly, from the Associated Press, writing for the *Washington Times*, Matt Decker for his installment of 'Syria: A Nation in Crisis.'"

* * *

Matt felt time stand still when the presenter announced him as the winner and he stood to walk to the podium. He accepted his award and leaned toward the microphone, taking a deep breath. "Thank you to the *New York Press* and to all of my colleagues, former and current. I appreciate this honor, especially for doing something I care so deeply about." He looked straight at Elizabeth. From that distance, and with the blinding lights, he couldn't tell if she was looking back. "Uh, again, thank you. This was one of my more difficult assignments, not just because of the peril I found myself in but because when I started working in Syria, I had no idea what was going to happen. Sometimes that's how life is: you take it one day at a time, and when you find yourself in the middle of a war . . . or even an awkward situation, you don't react; you respond and make the most of what occurs."

The room erupted in applause, but Matt could only focus on the figure fleeing from the room. He rushed after her, much to the chagrin of the beautiful model who was supposed to lead recipients off the stage in an organized fashion.

"Elizabeth, wait!" he yelled, bumping his way through tables and haphazardly placed chairs.

He found her leaning against the railing of the dock.

"Elizabeth," he said, placing a hand on her shoulder. She flinched. "Please look at me." He sat his statue down and made her turn around. "I wanted to tell you, to explain before this happened. But I didn't know how."

Tears pooled in her eyes, which she tried to mask with anger. "Why should you care if I look like a fool? I mean, you're just a *client*, right? You don't owe me anything."

Her words stung. "Is that all I am? I guess your friend was right."

Now his words seemed to have found their way home. "I know Melissa told Tyler about our bet."

"Yeah, so talk about who has made who look like a fool."

"Whom," she added, her reward a slight smile.

"Is that all it was?" he asked after a moment's silence.

Elizabeth shrugged. "At first. I wanted so badly to prove to everyone that what I did had validity, that it meant something." She lowered her head. "That *I* meant something. But then all that changed."

"Did it?" he lifted her chin.

"Of course."

Matt let out a groan and began to pace. "What a mess we've made. But I know how we can solve it." He walked back to her and held out his hand. "Hello, my name's Matt Decker. I'm a freelance reporter, formerly working for the *Washington Post* and currently on assignment with the *New York Times*. I was born and raised in Austin, Texas, but I haven't lived there for about three years. My mom and dad still live there. I have two brothers and a sister . . . who really is very determined. But, no, I don't live on a ranch, and I've never ridden a horse in my life, which made our outing this morning even more adventurous. Anyway, I make my way around the country, bumming off of friends who live in the areas where I work, and this is the way I normally speak, with the exception of an occasional 'ya'll.' Now it's your turn."

Elizabeth turned away from him as she spoke. "My name's Elizabeth Harding. I grew up in Brooklyn, New York, with my mom and dad. At least, until they got divorced when I was fifteen. Then it was my mom and me for a few years. We did all right for a while until we had to move to a pretty rough neighborhood in Bushwick because my dad wasn't very consistent with paying the child support." Her voice cracked a little. "My mom worked two jobs, so I rarely saw her. I haven't seen my dad since."

"One day some Mormon missionaries came to our door and started teaching us about God's plan for us. I'd never thought about having a plan for my life—it was always more about survival. But I liked what I heard, and after a few months, I got baptized. Going to church gave me the answers I was looking for," she said, her tone brightening. "I wanted so badly for my mom to know what I'd found, but instead, she found her answers at the bottom of a wine bottle. By then I couldn't take her drinking and neglect any longer, so after high school, I moved out and found a few friends who'd take me in while I went to paralegal school.

After I graduated, I moved here to Manhattan. I met Andrea, and at first we lived in an apartment the size of a closet, but we took care of each other, and eventually I found work at a law office. It wasn't easy, but working with those attorneys, I realized how important it was to know how to speak and be articulate. So I went back to school, took some more classes, and here I am." She turned around and threw up her arms. "I know it sounds stupid, but I guess I figured if I could sound differently, maybe I could be different and put the past behind me." Her shoulders crumpled as she finished.

Matt wrapped his arms around her and spoke quietly. "It's okay. You don't have to put the past behind you, because it's made you who you are: a beautiful, strong, and courageous woman. And I don't care where you're from. I'm more interested in where you're going."

Wiping her tears away, Elizabeth started to protest. "But we're so different, and I don't know how—"

Matt cut her off. "We're not as different as you think. I was a missionary in Tennessee several years ago. And you thought *I* had an accent! Elizabeth, in a city of millions, do you really think it was a coincidence that we met? As for how to go about this . . ." He winked. "I reckon we can larn how to do it together, ma'am. If you're willing to trust me."

"Hey, are you two all right?"

They turned to see Melissa, Andrea, and Tyler in the doorway.

Elizabeth wiped her eyes. "We're fine. In fact, I think we're more than fine."

"Good." Melissa smirked. "I thought you were out here celebrating because you'd won the bet."

Matt shook his head. "Nah, I'm pretty sure I'm the person who won."

Elizabeth put her hand in his. "I think we both won."

Epilogue

Six months later

"WHERE ARE WE GOING NOW?" Elizabeth asked.

Matt groaned. "For the last time, you'll find out when we get there."

This time they didn't need to take a taxi, because Jean-Georges' was right across the street from Central Park.

As they crossed from Columbus Circle, Elizabeth laughed. "I think we're a little overdressed for Rollerblading in Central Park.

"Nope, no Rollerblading this time."

"Bicycling?"

"Not even close."

Elizabeth had no choice but to follow along. Matt had just taken her to a very expensive dinner to celebrate the half-year anniversary of when they'd met, though they should have been celebrating his new full-time position at the *New York Times*. She'd told Matt they didn't need to do anything that extravagant for something so insignificant, but then he'd reminded her that his grandpap had told him that any milestone in a relationship was worth celebrating extravagantly—it was why his grandparents had stayed married for sixty years.

They stopped right inside the entryway to the park. As she looked around, she saw that the familiar ice cream cart now served hot chocolate. "Ahh, I figured it out. Now you want some dessert. As long as we don't get run over this time."

"Not quite." Matt wiped his hands on his suit pants and then put one hand into his suit coat pocket. "Six months ago we had a wonderful day here."

"That's true. And a lot has happened since then. You have a fabulous job to look forward to. Andrea has a real shot at becoming a weekday anchor. And, alas, Tyler almost convinced Melissa to go back to school instead of taking that modeling job out in Los Angeles. If only they knew what they were missing," she said, giving him a gentle kiss.

"That reminds me of another kiss—a kiss I'll never forget." Matt looked at her so intently it made her blush. "After that, things got a little rocky because you had this theory—"

"You're never going to let me forget that, are you?"

"Hardly, because I don't want to forget. You told your friends you could tell a person's future by the words they say. So here it goes." He knelt on the sidewalk, taking his hand out of his pocket and holding up a ring. "Will you marry me?"

Elizabeth stood there, speechless. She couldn't believe it was finally happening.

"I hope this isn't a total surprise . . . If you need more time," he stammered.

"The exact theory was that it only took three words," she interrupted him. "You used four." She laughed. "I guess it's up to me to do this right." She pulled him up to his feet and kissed him, much to the enjoyment of the crowd that had gathered around them. Then she whispered in his ear, "I love you."

The crowd cheered as they kissed again.

"I have one more surprise," Matt said with a smile as he put the ring on her finger. They heard the clip-clop of a horse behind them, and Matt turned and waved at the familiar carriage driver who pulled up beside them.

"You two love birds need a ride across the pahk?" he said as he twirled his mustache. "Free of chahge again."

Matt ushered Elizabeth over to the carriage and helped her in with a laugh. "Should I drive the carriage again?"

The horse gave an immediate neigh, to which Elizabeth added, "Not this time. I think I'll be much safer if you're back here with me."

Matt laughed. "And trust me, I'll be much happier."

About the Author

K.C. GRANT IS THE AUTHOR of three published books with Covenant: *Abish: Daughter of God*, *Abish: Mother of Faith*, and *Venom*. She has also had two short stories published in Covenant's Christmas anthologies and has written numerous magazine and newspaper articles. She is a member of LDStorymakers and, in her spare time, loves to travel, design her dream house, and spend time with her husband and two beautiful girls. Visit her at www.kcgrantwriterscorner.blogspot.com.

K.C. GRANT HAS ALSO WRITTEN

Abish: Daughter of God
Abish: Mother of Faith
Venom

A Crying Shame

Aubrey Mace

To my girls, who dragged me to Paint Nite,
where I had a marvelous time, even though I have
the artistic talent of a five-year-old.

And to Grandma Dawna—
yes, this is the story with Max in it. ☺

Chapter One

I'D SPENT THE LAST FORTY-NINE minutes pulled over on the side of the road, crying.

It wasn't the kind of thing I did—ever. But this was a special circumstance.

I fumbled in the glove box and found several unused napkins from various fast-food restaurants that Past Me had very kindly squirreled away for Present Me to take advantage of in an event such as this. I used them to mop my face and told myself to snap out of it. I was done crying. This was a fluke. Tears were a foreign concept to me.

My phone rang, and my heart slammed into my throat. Maybe it was Colby. It had to be Colby. I scrambled for it, knocking it onto the floor. When I picked it up, I was disappointed to see that it was only Elle.

"Hello?" I said. I felt like I was mostly in control of the flood of tears now, but I was surprised by how quavery my voice was.

"Cass, where are you? The movie's starting!" Elle hissed through the phone. Before I could answer, I heard her talking to someone else. "Yeah, so what? It's the previews. Lighten up!"

"I'm not coming," I said. I tried to think of the simplest explanation that would get Elle off the phone the quickest. If she was already growling at someone in the theater, it wasn't a good sign. Elle was the best, most loyal friend in the world, but she had a temper that ignited quicker than flipping on a light switch.

"What? I already bought the tickets! You have to come!"

"I can't. I'm sorry." I could feel the tears lurking just below the surface. Any little thing might set them off again. As someone who never cried, I was mystified by this. I'd been crying for a solid forty-nine minutes before this. How could there possibly be *more* tears?

"You sound funny. Are you sick?"

"I'm not sick." I should have said I was sick. That would have been the easy explanation.

"What's wrong? Something's wrong. I can tell."

"It's Colby." My voice broke on his name, and the tears were back. This was so embarrassing. I had no control over it.

"What happened?"

"I can't talk about it. It's stupid."

"Are you crying?" she asked.

"Maybe."

"You never cry. What happened?" she repeated. I felt like I was on the stand, being questioned by a particularly voracious prosecutor in a brutal court case.

"I told him I loved him."

"And?"

"And . . . nothing. That was it. Because he didn't say it b-b-b-back," I sobbed. My confession must have been the breaking point. This was now well beyond what could be handled by a couple of spare glove-box napkins.

"What did he say?" Elle demanded.

"He said, 'You're a great girl.' And he hugged meeeeee," I wailed.

"Where are you?"

"I'm parked on the side of the road across the street from Baskin Robbins."

"Okay, don't go anywhere. I'm coming." Before she could hang up the phone, I heard her snap at what I could only guess was the same person from earlier. "Yes, I'm leaving. *I'm leaving.* Are you happy now?"

I hit the end button on the call so I wouldn't have to know what happened. I supposed if Elle didn't show up, I'd get a call to come bail her out of jail. This idea afforded me a tiny smile. It wasn't like she'd ever been in jail before, at least not that I knew about. But it wasn't entirely out of the realm of possibility.

Chapter Two

"Well, this was a convenient place for you to have this little breakdown," Elle commented.

It was a Saturday afternoon, and Baskin Robbins was pretty busy. I'd managed to stop crying long enough to come inside, but I still felt self-conscious. My eyes were red, and my face felt puffy. Of course there had to be a line. It was probably just my imagination, but I felt like everyone was looking at me.

"I didn't plan on falling apart, but I'm glad you approve of the location," I said. "I don't even like ice cream."

"Seriously?"

"I've told you that a million times!"

"Yeah, but I sort of thought it was like those girls who say they don't like pizza so they have an excuse not to eat it in social settings, but really they love it and they're afraid of getting fat."

"No, I genuinely don't like ice cream."

Elle was the most practical person I'd ever met, except for one thing—she carried a Magic 8 ball with her absolutely *everywhere* and consulted it on a regular basis. She pulled it out of her massive purse and asked, "Does Cass like ice cream?" She waited for the response. "My sources say no," she read aloud.

"I told you."

"Then what are we doing here?"

"Society states that when a woman is unhappy, she should seek out ice cream in mass quantities. I thought I should try it."

"You're weird."

I gave her a tiny smile. "I know. But you love me."

She put the Magic 8 ball back in her bag. "I can't believe you actually shed tears. When was the last time you cried about something?"

"My dog got ran over. I was six. Or seven, maybe."

She shook her head. "This is very peculiar. Tell me what happened."

"I already told you what happened."

She rolled her eyes. "No, I want the extended version."

"You want more details about my complete and total humiliation?"

"What happened after he hugged you?"

"That was it."

"That couldn't be it. He hugged you, and you were magically transported to your car, where you proceeded to melt down?"

"No."

She folded her arms across her chest. "Well?"

"After he hugged me and I realized he really wasn't going to say it back, I left."

"You just left? Without saying anything?"

I shrugged. "What was there to say? 'Just kidding? I take it back? Please don't panic and dump me?'"

"How about, 'You're obviously a big jerk, and I couldn't love you if you were the last man on the planet'?" Elle suggested.

"You know, it's funny, but in the moment, my brain wasn't really equipped to come up with something like that."

She handed me her phone. "Tell him now."

"I have a phone." I took it out of my pocket and waved it at her just to prove the point.

"Of course you do. But you're not going to use it." She grabbed my phone. "Here, I'll do it."

I grabbed it back. "You are not going to text my boyfriend and tell him what a jerk he is."

"Someone should. We need to decide what we want. It's almost our turn," she said.

"Since I don't like ice cream, I'm not sure it matters."

We started scanning through the thirty-one flavors on the menu board. Elle made a face. "Eeew. Who eats rum raisin ice cream?"

"That does sound particularly bad. Ugh. Who eats orange sherbet?"

"Hey, I like orange sherbet," Elle said. "How about chocolate chip cookie dough?"

"No, thanks. I don't want salmonella."

"I think that's a myth. Besides, it's not like you're eating an entire tube of raw cookie dough."

"I'll pass."

"Pistachio almond?" she asked.

"Only two kinds of nuts? Please. I require at least four varieties in every scoop." Despite the terrible day thus far, I was actually having a good time. Maybe people were right about ice cream.

"I think I'm getting peanut butter and banana," Elle said.

"Really?"

"What's wrong with that?"

"Nothing, I guess. I thought you were making it up."

"It's right there," she said, pointing to the sign. "Have you decided what you want?"

"Not peanut butter and banana."

It was our turn at the counter.

"What can I get for you ladies today?" the scooping guy asked with a smile. Something about him reminded me of Colby. I think it was his eyes. Inexplicably the tears sprang into action again. This was getting ridiculous. Was I doomed to have this reaction for the rest of my life anytime someone or something reminded me of my boyfriend/ex-boyfriend? I wasn't even sure what to call him anymore.

"I have to go," I muttered, bolting for the door.

"What should I get you?" Elle yelled.

"I don't care!" I yelled back.

Chapter Three

WHEN ELLE REJOINED ME IN the car, she handed me a giant cup of ice cream studded with a variety of chocolate.

"Thanks," I said, sniffing and willing the tears to go away.

"Next time we go in there, it's my turn to start bawling. Look at the size of your ice cream compared to mine! That guy obviously felt sorry for you."

"See? It's a well-known stereotype that crying women need ice cream. And chocolate. So this is actually a double stereotype." I dipped the spoon in and licked at it without much enthusiasm.

"Are you saying you don't want all of that? Even the chocolate?"

"I'm saying I resent the world for telling me ice cream will fix everything."

Elle laughed, and then I laughed too because it was such a silly thing to say.

"What are you going to do about Colby?" she asked finally, when the laughter had died down.

Two more tears rolled down my cheeks without any warning. I planted my plastic spoon deep into the ice cream. I didn't trust myself to say anything.

"Do you really love him?" Elle asked.

"I hope you got napkins," I said.

Elle pulled a giant stack of them out of her bag. It looked like she'd emptied the dispenser. I set the ice cream on the dashboard, blotted at my eyes with a couple of napkins, then put my head in my hands. Whether I loved Colby seemed too sad to even consider now that he'd rejected me.

"Does Cass love Colby?" Elle asked her trusty Magic 8 ball that she'd hauled back out of her bag. There was a long pause.

I sat up and looked at her. "What did it say?"

"'Reply hazy, try again.'"

"How appropriate."

"So do you?"

More tears. There seemed to be no end to them. But these weren't the sobbing, choking tears of earlier. These were like ants moving cookie crumbs; they still had a purpose, but they went about their business without making a big fuss about it.

"Do you?" Elle repeated. I think she was starting to worry that I might retreat into some catatonic state where I'd be permanently unreachable.

"I think so. It's hard to say. I've never said it to anyone before, you know? And that brief but intensely painful experience didn't exactly make me want to dig deeper and explore my feelings."

"Well, if you really love him, you should talk to him about it. But if you have any doubts, any doubts *at all*, I think you should dump him immediately."

"How am I supposed to dump him when I'm pretty sure he's already dumped me?"

She shrugged. "Maybe you dumped him first. It's his word against yours."

"Elle!"

"What? He's obviously a terrible person. What kind of guy doesn't say 'I love you' back?"

I sighed. "The kind that doesn't love you back."

She paused for a minute, then got this look on her face that said she was about to say something incredibly profound. "Are you going to eat that or what?" she said.

Or . . . not.

I unearthed the spoon and studied the chocolatey, rapidly melting mess. "Of course I'm going to eat it. I'm a woman scorned, and this is what the world says I should be doing." I took a huge bite and tasted it carefully, considering. "Nope. Still don't like ice cream."

Elle sneaked her spoon into my cup and stole a bite. "It's delicious. You're weird."

"Yeah, but you love me."

She smiled at me fondly. "I do love you."

"See! At least someone can say it."

Chapter Four

I couldn't call Colby.

A tiny part of me hoped when I got home from Baskin Robbins a week ago that he'd be on my doorstep with a dozen roses and a grand apology. But after all these days, there was still no sign of him. I was going to have to accept that it was really over. I'd put myself out there, and he'd panicked. If he wanted to talk to me, he knew where to find me. I couldn't embarrass myself any further by chasing him if he wasn't interested. Besides, I couldn't stop crying at the most inconvenient moments. The slightest thing could set me off with no warning, and the last thing I wanted to do was cry in front of him. I wasn't about to let him know how much he'd hurt me.

Maybe three months was too soon to tell someone you loved them, but how was I supposed to know? I was completely new at this. I'd never said it before. Well, not to a boy anyway. And it's not like there was a love manual or something . . . except there probably was. Elle has always said you can buy anything on Amazon.

I searched Amazon just for the heck of it and found several books telling men how to understand women and three times that number telling women how to understand men and several hundred other books that should probably contain some sort of warning for explicit content. Perhaps I should have worded my search differently.

How in the world was anyone supposed to know if the person they were seeing was *the one*?

Colby. Sigh. He had beautiful green eyes, and he was smart, and he seemed to like spending time with me. I was reasonably sure I loved him a week after we met, so I thought I'd shown remarkable restraint waiting this long. All my friends were getting engaged. Well, except Elle—she was militantly single. She liked going out and having a good time, but she didn't want to commit to anyone, and the idea of trotting out the *L* word triggered a reaction that was almost anaphylactic.

I, on the other hand, was ready to be in love. I wanted to be the one getting engaged. I thought it was only a matter of time before Colby popped the question and I joined the ranks of girls who seemed to spend every spare minute planning their impending nuptials. Instead I was hunkered down in my apartment, watching *The Lake House* with a massive cup of herbal tea that had long ago turned cold and an economy-sized box of Kleenex. It looked more like I had the flu than a broken heart.

Maybe Colby just needed some time. It had been a week, but he could still come around. Once he had a chance to miss me, surely he'd be back, and I'd be ready to forgive him. If only I could stop crying. I'd never seen anything like this steady stream of tears. I'd spent most of the last week wondering if I had become chronically dehydrated. It was better when I was at work. If I was busy, my brain didn't have as much time to focus on my troubles. But home was a different story.

I blew my nose loudly and threw the Kleenex toward the wastebasket by the wall. I missed, and it joined a bunch of its buddies on the floor as evidence of my lack of ability at the free-throw line. Basketball never was my sport. It was late enough that I should start thinking about dinner, but I couldn't quite make myself care enough to do anything about it.

There was a knock at my door. Colby. It had to be Colby coming to apologize. And I was a mess in every possible way.

I ran to the mirror and stared into it in despair. I was in my best little black dress—it had become a very uncomfortable uniform. I wanted to look nice if Colby showed up, but it never occurred to me until now that it might look odd if I was just sitting around the house in formal wear. My mascara was smeared from crying, my hair was sticking out in weird places, and my eyes were bloodshot. What to do? I couldn't go to the door looking like this.

The knocking was more persistent now. "I know you're in there, Cass. Open up."

Elle. It was just Elle. I didn't know if I was relieved or incredibly disappointed. I had this picture in my head of Colby swinging me into his arms and kissing me repeatedly, all while telling me what a fool he'd been and promising never to leave me again.

Elle had been out of town since the day after the Colby debacle. She'd been calling and texting to check up on me, but I didn't think she understood how bad it was. She was supposed to get back today—I should have known she'd come here and should have disposed of all the Kleenex evidence accordingly. I didn't want Elle to see me like this either, but it wasn't like she was going to dump me. Probably. I opened the door a crack and prepared for the inevitable deluge of criticism.

"Hey," I said, hiding behind the door.

"I thought I was going to have to break the door down."

I laughed. If I passed the saneness test, maybe she'd go away. "How was your trip?" I asked.

"It was great."

"Lots of sun?"

"Boatloads of sun. Are you going to let me in?" she demanded.

So much for that plan. "That depends. Are you going to be nice?"

"Why wouldn't I be nice? I'm always nice. I exude nice."

I opened the door, mainly because I knew there was no chance of her going away. Elle came inside and surveyed my apartment.

"Wow," she said finally. "It looks like a crime scene in here." She walked over to the wastebasket and pointed at the Kleenex grave-yard. "Yes, I believe we can say without a doubt that this was where Cassandra's will to live perished. Time of death? Judging from the amount of Kleenex, I'd say approximately one week ago."

"Haha," I said.

"Are you going somewhere?" she asked, giving me a strange look.

"Uh, I was cleaning out my closet. I'm going to give some old clothes away, so I was trying them on first to see if they fit." Which I thought was a pretty convincing story on the fly.

Realization dawned on her face. "Oh, Cass. You got dressed up in case Colby came by, didn't you? Have you been wearing this every day?"

"No," I said stubbornly. Then I sighed because I knew I wasn't fooling anyone, least of all my best friend. "Yesterday I had on a red dress."

"I guess I know now why you didn't want to FaceTime. But that one looks great on you," Elle said. "You should wear it every day."

I laughed, and I loved her even more in that moment for not calling me out on what was obviously the behavior of a crazy person.

"Well, I can't afford to take you anywhere looking like that. Get dressed in some less fancy clothes—we're going out," she said.

Chapter Five

I SAT ON THE COUCH and tried to disappear under my favorite faux fur blanket. "You just got back. You must be tired, and I don't really feel like going out tonight."

"I'm not tired at all, and your clothing says otherwise," Elle said. "I've already made plans for us—plans that involved prepaying. So you're going to have to be a good sport and come with me, I'm afraid. I knew you'd need some cheering up, but I had no idea the situation was so dire."

"You should have called first."

"If I'd called first, you would have said no." And she was right.

"Hence the surprise attack?" I asked.

"Exactly."

Going out was the absolute last thing I wanted to do tonight. I'd rather have minor outpatient surgery; at least I could take the blanket with me to that. But Elle had that resolute look that said I might as well just give in now and avoid a lengthy argument because the final outcome would be the same either way.

Only this time I wasn't having it. I was an adult, and if I wanted to stay home and sprawl on the couch, that was what I was going to do. "I'm not going," I said. I tightened my grip on the blanket, and Elle's eyes narrowed.

"You're like Linus with that blanket. Don't make me forcibly remove it."

"You wouldn't."

"Wouldn't I? Trust me when I say you don't want to test that theory." She took a step toward me, and I started to fear for the fate of the blanket.

I flung it off myself and dropped it on the couch. "All right, calm down. You're such a drill sergeant sometimes."

"You'll thank me later. You have twenty minutes to make yourself look presentable."

I held my arms out to my sides. "This is as ready as I'm gonna get."

"You're a little too ready. And your mascara says you just lost your best friend. Go."

"I have to check on something first," I said.

"Now you're just stalling."

"I'm not stalling! There is something I genuinely have to do." I went to the fridge and got out a bag of premixed salad.

Elle folded her arms across her chest. "I can't wait to see where you're going with this. Do you urgently need a snack before we leave?"

"No, but George does." I put some of the salad in a little bowl.

"This is so much worse than I thought. Did you get an imaginary friend who likes salad while I was gone?"

"George is the guinea pig I brought home from work. I'm taking care of her for a while."

"George is a her?"

"I hope so. She's very pregnant."

Elle groaned. "Cass, I thought we agreed you weren't bringing any more desperate animals home!"

"But look at her!" I said, pointing to the cage.

"Where is she?"

"She's hiding in the little house over there." I'd cut a door in the side of a plastic tub and turned it upside down to make George a hiding spot, and she spent most of her time in there. When I put down the bowl of salad, she waddled out and started eating a sliced carrot with almost alarming speed. "You can pet her if you want."

"I'll think about it and get back to you," Elle said.

"Awww, but she's such a little sweeter. I couldn't leave her there to possibly have her babies all alone at night when everyone's gone home." I scratched George behind the ears while she continued to mow her way through the salad.

"She's an animal. That's what they do."

"But guinea pigs have a hard time giving birth. It's dangerous for them."

"So what are you going to do—massage her little feet and give her plenty of ice chips?" Elle said.

I glared at her. "George hasn't had an easy life. Someone left her at the clinic with a note—'Please take care of my guinea pig, George. I thought it was a boy, but my mom said it's going to have babies, so I guess it's not.'"

Elle laughed.

"It was so sad! That poor kid," I said.

"You need a different job, a less depressing one. Maybe something in retail where you get a nice discount."

"I happen to love my job."

"I know, I know. I'm not going to change your mind. Well, unless there are any other stray animals lurking around your apartment that need dinner, you'd better hurry and change because now you only have ten minutes."

"I suppose it was too much to hope for that you'd get attached to George and not want to leave."

"Yes, that was definitely a stretch. Off you go." She shooed me in the direction of my bedroom.

Chapter Six

I felt slightly more normal with jeans and a sweater on, but I still didn't want to go. I gazed longingly at my abandoned blanket on the couch as Elle herded me out the door.

"I changed my mind!" I said, looking for something sturdy to anchor myself to.

"I thought you might say that. Which is why I brought you something special."

I smiled. "A bribe?"

"Something like that."

"What is it?"

"Goldfish."

"Shut. Up." Ever since I was a little kid, there was nothing that cheered me up like a couple of goldfish. Elle knew just how to toy with me. "Goldfish? Really? Where?"

"In the car."

"But it's too cold for them out there!"

"Then you better hurry," she said.

I pushed past her and ran downstairs to her car, peering in the locked doors. "I don't see any goldfish."

"You get them at the end of the night, for being a good sport."

I considered this for a minute. "There are no goldfish, are there?"

"You'll never know if you don't play along."

"I have to get my gloves from my car," I said.

"You have two minutes. We're going to be late."

"It's freezing, and I'm not going anywhere without my gloves. Take it or leave it."

Elle sighed. "Get your gloves, tiny frozen creature."

I went to my car and opened the door, then leaned across the seat to grab my gloves when I saw something on the windshield. There was a paper tucked under the wiper.

I snatched it, and there was my name on the front in Colby's handwriting. My full name—Cassandra, not Cass, like everyone called me. Like he always called me.

This couldn't be good.

I unfolded it and read it quickly. It was almost unthinkably brief—*You're a wonderful person, but I'm not looking for a commitment, wish you every happiness, have a nice life.* I'd like to say I was so upset I couldn't finish reading it, but it wasn't long enough for the shock to even have a chance to kick in. I didn't have to work today, so I hadn't left the house since the day before. Which meant that sometime between last night when I got home and this moment, Colby had been here, mere feet away from where I'd been waiting for him. I thought if I stayed at home, I'd definitely be here if he happened to come by. I had no idea I should have been waiting in the car instead.

"What's the holdup? Are you knitting those gloves?" Elle shouted from her car.

I was glad I hadn't bothered with the new mascara because I was already crying again. I walked over to her car woodenly and handed her the letter. It took her all of five seconds to read it.

"You've got to be kidding me. Where was this?" she asked.

"On the windshield."

"I can't believe it. This is all you get?"

"Apparently."

"And you're crying again. You don't cry." Elle looked genuinely alarmed.

"I know. I never cried until this week, and now I can't stop. It's like I'm broken. Colby broke me!"

"Oh, no. You're not broken. I will not allow him to break you." The letter appeared to be getting quite crumpled as she shook it in her fist over her head. Her face was dangerously red. I've often thought that Elle needed one of those emergency safety valves you could turn to let off steam so when the pressure got too high no permanent damage was done. "See? This. This right here is why we're going out. Colby isn't worth this flood of tears since he couldn't even be bothered to break up with you in person. What kind of a guy breaks up with a girl he's been dating for two months—"

"Three months," I interrupted miserably.

"*Three* months. With a note. That's one tiny step above ending a relationship with a text." She realized she was mangling my note and tried to smooth it out before handing it back to me. "You've got to let this go, Cass. You deserve so much more than this."

Tears were still leaking from the corners of my eyes. I couldn't do this. Not now. "I'm going back upstairs. Thanks for trying. Maybe we can go out next week, okay?"

"No, not okay. You've been moping in your apartment for a week, and it's time to face the world again."

"I'm not ready."

"You need to do this now because if you don't, it'll just get easier and easier to stay home until finally you're one of those people who never leaves the house and has their groceries delivered."

"Do you know any place that does that? Because grocery delivery sounds handy."

Elle glared at me.

"Fine, let's get this over with. Where are we going?"

She smiled, a mix of mystery and pure evil. "You'll see."

"That sounds ominous."

"It's all in your perspective."

Chapter Seven

THE HIGHER WE DROVE INTO the mountains, the more snow there was. I hated snow.

"If you really wanted to cheer me up, you'd take me somewhere with beaches and eighty-degree weather," I said.

"I love you, Cass, and I want you to be happy, but my cheering-up budget doesn't include airfare. I just got back from vacation, and I'm broke."

"Are you taking me to some sort of mountain retreat so I can eat kale and tree bark and find myself?" I asked.

Elle snorted. "Please. Do I seem like the kind of hippy-dippy person who would inflict that on you?"

"It's the middle of winter, and its freezing. The only thing to do at this altitude is ski, and you know I hate skiing."

"Since you went one-on-one with the giant pine tree, I know. We're not going skiing."

I was relieved, but at the same time, I wondered if I hadn't traded a bad fate for a worse one. "My fish better not be sloshing around in your trunk."

"Your little fishies are perfectly safe . . . for now."

When Elle parked the car at a ski resort, my heart started doing flip flops in my chest. "You said no skiing! You promised!"

"Relax, Miss Broken Femur 2006; we're not skiing."

By the time we got inside, I was shivering and stamping the snow from my shoes. We took the elevator to the top floor, where as far as I could see, the only thing up there was a swank restaurant.

"I should have left the dress on. We can't afford this," I hissed.

Elle grabbed my shoulders like it was all she could do not to shake me senseless. "Cass, do you trust me?"

"Sometimes."

"That'll have to do. I know that spontaneity is not one of your special gifts, but I need you to just roll with it for the next couple of hours."

"Couple of *hours*?" I squeaked.

"May I help you?" the man at the desk asked.

"We're here for Paint Nite," Elle said.

"Excellent. Right this way, please," he said. We followed him through the restaurant to a room in the back with a breathtaking wall of windows. There were two long tables in the center of the room with lots of canvases and paint and brushes set up.

I sucked in a deep breath. "This . . . is a bad idea."

"I knew you would say that, which is precisely why I didn't tell you where we were going."

"I can't do this," I said, shaking my head. "You know I have absolutely no artistic talent whatsoever."

There was a waitress making the rounds to people already sitting at the tables, taking drink and food orders. One woman sipped a glass of wine.

"Why are they all drinking?" I whispered in Elle's direction, probably too loudly.

She shrugged. "Some people need a little loosening up, I guess."

"I'm not drinking!" I said, this time definitely too loudly.

"Of course we're not drinking. I don't expect you to drink. But I do expect you to paint."

"I told you, I can't paint," I said.

"Everyone can paint. You just don't know it yet," a voice said over my shoulder. I turned around to see a smiling woman wearing a Paint Nite apron. She stuck out her hand for me to shake. "Hi, I'm Chelly. I'm your instructor tonight. You seem a bit tense. Did you get dragged here?"

"I got tricked here," I said. "How could you tell?"

"It's the look of betrayal on your face. There's always one in every class," she explained. "Trust me, you have nothing to worry about. I'm going to walk you through it step by step. Even the nervous ones have a good time, I promise. Find a seat, and order a drink if you want." She left to talk to some of the other potential painters.

"See?" Elle said as if this explanation made everything okay.

I was unconvinced. "I can't paint," I repeated.

"Look, you need to calm down for a minute and listen to me. You deserve a night out with no worries so you can remember what it's like to have fun."

I laughed at her bizarre idea of a good time. "Fun? This isn't fun—this is the complete exact opposite of fun. This is where ulcers are born."

Elle led me toward the nearest chair and pushed me into it. "You are going to sit in that chair and paint a picture and have a good time doing it. Is that understood?"

I sighed. I wasn't getting out of this. "Whatever," I said, scowling. "But you owe me for this big-time."

"Excuse me, but I think you're in my chair," a male voice said.

Chapter Eight

ELLE GLARED AT THE REDHEADED guy who was still smiling pleasantly enough. Apparently he wasn't getting the there-are-only-two-seats-left-at-this-end-of-the-table-and-we're-sitting-here-so-beat-it vibe she was hurtling in his direction. She kicked her glare up a notch, but he still didn't move. I bit my lip so I wouldn't grin. He must either be very brave or completely clueless.

"We're sitting here. Is this going to be a problem?" Elle growled. I wondered why everything with Elle had to come down to life or death.

"It's okay, we can move," I said, standing up.

"We're not moving," Elle said.

"It's all right," the guy said, smiling. He had one of those easy grins, like everything in life amused him. I couldn't imagine how he was still managing to be friendly in the face of Elle's wrath. "I can see that you're attached to these seats. I'll move." He walked around to the other side of the table and stood at the chair across from me. "When the waitress comes back with my drink, will you send her my way?" he said. He was still smiling, and I couldn't help smiling back at his joke, like he was moving to another country where the waitress would never find him without a forwarding address instead of across the table.

Elle paused for a moment, and I could tell she was mulling something over. "What's your name?" she asked the guy. The scowl was gone.

"Max," he said easily.

"Okay, Max. You sit here," she said, pulling me up and pointing to the seat I'd been sitting in. "And you sit here," she said to me, replanting me in the one next to it.

"Uh, where are you going to sit?" I asked her.

Elle walked over the seat Max had been about to occupy on the other side of the table. "I'm going to sit here."

"It's okay, really," Max said. "You sit with your friend. I don't mind."

"I prefer the light over here," Elle said, which sounded like a perfectly reasonable argument if you were a professional artist. But I knew Elle, and there was only one reason she'd make up a story like that: she was up to something.

"Okay, I'll sit over there with you if the light's so great," I said. Two could play at that game.

"Sorry—only one chair," she said, smiling sweetly.

It was true. There was a coat draped over the back of the chair next to her. I couldn't believe she was doing this to me. First she dragged me here to paint when she knew I had no talent, and then she abandoned me to some stranger all night. Sometimes it was hard to remember why we were friends.

Elle reached across the table and grabbed Max's hand before he could do anything about it. "Max, I'm Elle."

"It's nice to meet you, Elle," he said. His eyes seemed to indicate he was amused, which was not the usual reaction when someone met Elle for the first time. Most people were annoyed. It took a while for Elle to grow on people, like one of those mushrooms you'd find growing on the back of a log in the darkest part of the woods—you knew it would be delicious, but at the same time, there was a good chance it could kill you. She sat down in her chair and busied herself pretending to inspect her brushes, as though they were weapons she was familiarizing herself with in case she had to use them in battle.

Max was amused. I was annoyed.

Chapter Nine

Max turned to me. "And you are?"

"Cassandra," I said. "But no one calls me that."

"Okay, what do people call you?"

"Cass."

"What should I call you?"

"Cass is fine."

Max sat in his chair. I snuck a peek at Elle through the slot between the canvases, and she gave me a sneaky smile before she went back to studying her brushes.

"Will you excuse me for a minute?" I said to Max.

"Certainly," he said.

I stood and went around to the other side of the table. "Let's go find the restroom," I said to Elle.

"I don't have to go," she said.

"Oh, I think you do." I motioned toward the door with my head, and she gave me a questioning look, so I did it again more forcefully, widening my eyes at the same time. There could be no doubt as to what I wanted at this point, yet she persisted with the charade of confusion. I was starting to feel like we were in an episode of *I Love Lucy*, and I expected to hear the laugh track in the background any moment.

Elle finally rolled her eyes and stood. She gave Max an apologetic smile, which was bizarre, as I hustled her out of the room. I couldn't remember the last time Elle had apologized in any form for anything.

"What's going on in there?" I demanded once we were an acceptable distance from the door.

"I'm trying to help you, even though you're doing your best to sabotage things."

"Trying to help me by what—leaving me adrift in a class of strangers to do something I'm clueless about?"

"With a guy who likes you, yes. That was my intention."

"He doesn't like me. He doesn't even know me."

"He was totally checking you out. He couldn't keep his eyes off you."

"Only because I was sitting in his seat. This is your big plan? Honestly?"

"He's interested," she insisted. "I never once saw Colby look at you like that in the whole two months you dated."

"Three months. And you're delusional."

Elle checked her cell phone. "Okay, it's 7:05. Give it until 8:30. If you're not convinced by then, I'll switch places with you."

"I'll still be alone!"

"Fine, if you're not having a good time by 8:30, we'll take our sad little half-finished paintings and leave. Satisfied?"

I made her shake on it. Elle had a terrible habit of magically forgetting deals she made, but she never broke an actual promise.

Chapter Ten

WHEN I RETURNED TO MY seat, Max was drinking something that looked like champagne.

"I ordered you a drink," he said. "I hope you don't mind."

"I don't drink, thank you."

"I don't drink either."

"What's that?" I said, pointing to his glass.

"What does it look like?"

"Champagne."

He laughed. "People generally don't drink champagne over ice or through a straw. It's ginger ale."

I couldn't help laughing as well. "As you can see, I'm not really up on my straw versus no-straw beverages. I suppose I can handle ginger ale."

"And what do you do for a living? I'm going to take a wild guess and say you're not a bartender."

"I tried that, but I kept putting straws and ice in everything, so they had to let me go."

"So, why has your friend abandoned you, Cass?" Max asked.

I snorted before I could help it. *Nice, Cass. Very attractive.* "She does that—things she thinks are for my own good."

"And what are you supposed to learn from this situation?"

"She wants me to get out and have a good time. She thinks I've forgotten what fun is."

Max took another drink. "What led her to this conclusion?"

"I got out of a relationship about a week ago."

Unless it was my imagination, the smile on his face slipped a fraction, but he quickly covered it. Could Elle be right? Was this guy really interested in me? "Hmmm. Recently single. You have my condolences."

I couldn't tell from his tone if he was being genuine or sarcastic, and it still hurt too much to think about Colby being lost to me forever. "It's okay. I think maybe we'll still get back together."

"Oh. Right," Max said.

Elle kicked me under the table, and I winced.

Max laughed. "I take it she wasn't a fan of the ex."

"She's *nosy*," I said loudly, but I couldn't be sure whether she heard me, because that was when the music started—loud, upbeat music that was probably intended to boost people's confidence.

The server brought my ginger ale.

"Thank you," I said to Max.

He held up his glass. "To trying new things," he said.

My insides felt jumpy and as flimsy as cotton candy. I forced a smile. "New things," I repeated back.

We clinked glasses.

Chapter Eleven

"WHO'S READY TO GET STARTED?" Chelly asked. There was a general excited hum around the room, but my nervousness edged a little further into my throat.

"Everyone find a seat if you haven't already," she said. She was explaining the brushes and colors and how to mix them, and as scary as talking to Max was, it seemed the less frightening option at the moment.

"So, what are you doing here tonight?" I asked. I tried to keep the tentativeness from my voice but wasn't terribly successful. I noticed Elle give me an approving look through the crack in the canvases. I'd get even with her for this one day.

"Oh, I love Paint Nite," Max said. "I have fifty-three, no, fifty-four pictures from Paint Nite in my living room. Tonight will be number fifty-five."

I swallowed unnecessarily. "Really?"

"No."

I laughed. "Well, that's too bad. I was hoping that at least one of us knew what we were doing."

"Nope. Not a painter, I'm afraid. My mother gave me a Paint Nite Groupon for Christmas, so I felt obligated. She keeps asking to see the picture, and I thought I might as well get it over with. I think she's secretly hoping I'll be a painting prodigy and she'll be credited with discovering me."

"That was nice of you. My mother is a strictly gift-card-only sort of person, but if she had given me a Groupon for this, I think I would have conveniently lost it."

Max picked up the larger brush and played with the bristles. "Oh, not with my mother. There's no easy way out of these situations. She won't be satisfied until she's got the canvas hanging on her wall. There's her way and the hard way. I've learned it's much easier to just go along."

"Hmmm. I've always thought it was much easier to hide and hope the unpleasant thing went away."

Max looked up from the brush, his eyes latching directly onto mine. "And yet you're here."

I smiled, but I couldn't hold his gaze. It was too much. "I guess Elle is my version of your mother. It's easier to go along and get it over with."

"I heard that," Elle said from across the table.

I'd ordered french fries when the server had brought my drink, and I'd been so involved in talking to Max that I'd almost forgotten how hungry I was. When the server brought them, they were covered in parmesan cheese and some kind of herbs, and the minute I smelled them, my stomach growled like I hadn't eaten in a month.

"Those are some fancy fries," Max said.

"You want one?"

"Maybe. Do you mind?"

"Help yourself."

He took one and dipped it in the little side of ketchup, then chewed it thoughtfully. "I didn't know it was possible to dress up fries, but they've done it. It only needs one more thing."

"What would that be?"

"Mayonnaise."

I made a face. "You dip your fries in mayonnaise?"

"It's the perfect combination."

"You'll never convince me."

"Have you tried it?"

"I don't need to try it. It's unnatural."

The server was bringing drinks to the couple next to us, and Max tapped her on the shoulder. "Would you mind bringing her some mayonnaise?"

She gave him a strange look. "Okay."

"Great. She probably already thinks we're weird. We didn't order real drinks, and now you asked for mayonnaise," I said.

"Trust me. Once you've tried it, you'll never go back."

Chapter Twelve

I WAS SUPPOSED TO BE making three large gray triangle shapes on my canvas. Everyone else was done combining their white and black paint, but I only watched as they made triangle shapes with varying degrees of certainty. I was still caught in the fear/indecision of mixing. I figured if I kept making minute changes to the color, I could avoid committing myself indefinitely to putting paint on the canvas. I knew that as soon as I touched the brush to the surface, I would inevitably make a mistake, and there was no eraser. Paint was permanent.

While I made myself look busy mixing paint, I snuck periodic quick glances at Max's canvas, which he was beginning to cover with large strokes of gray. I admired and envied the ease with which his brush seemed to flow across the vast white expanse. I studied the canvas at the front of the room where the instructor was painting and tried to memorize the exact coordinates in case I managed to muster the courage to stop mixing paint and actually use some of it.

The music shifted seamlessly from one catchy pop song to the next. Everyone around me was painting and laughing, and I appeared to be the only person trapped in painting limbo.

"That's a really interesting interpretation you've got going on there," Max commented.

"You like it?" I said. "I call it *Snow-Covered Mountains in a Blizzard*."

Max whistled. "You're good at this. And I can see you've already picked a painting genre—you're obviously a minimalist."

I sighed. "This is harder than I thought."

"On the contrary, it's easier than I expected."

I gave him a skeptical look. "Go on; enlighten me."

"Well, when you look at the finished product, the idea of painting it seems really daunting. But when you break it down into easy steps, it doesn't seem so scary." Max dabbed his brush into the gray and used it to smooth out an uneven corner. "I can handle triangles. I've been handling triangles since kindergarten."

"When you say it like that, it sounds so simple. But when I look at my canvas, it's perfect now as it is. Anything I contribute will only muddy it."

"Or you might surprise yourself and create something fantastic. But you'll never know if you spend the rest of the night perfecting the paint-mixing process."

I gave him a dark look. "I think it needs a touch more black."

"If you start painting, I'll buy you dessert," Max said.

I stifled the part of me that was instantly thrilled at the idea of Max flirting with me. "I can't be bought."

"Well, you better do something. The instructor is coming."

He was right. The instructor was walking down the aisle on the other side of the table. It was only a matter of time before she made it around to this side and figured out I was using perpetual paint mixing to hide my paralyzing fear of painting. I took a deep breath and touched the brush to the blank canvas. Triangles were easy, I told myself, making a pyramid shape and filling it in with more gray.

When the instructor walked by, her eyes skimmed over my work, and she kept going. I let out a breath I didn't realize I was holding.

"See? That wasn't so hard," Max said.

"Mine doesn't look like the one at the front."

"That's because your triangles are floating. You need to paint all the way to the bottom." As soon as Max said it, I realized he was right.

"Maybe mine are magical floating mountains," I said.

"Hey, I'm just the guy with no vision, following instructions. Floating mountains are much more original."

It was nice of him to play along. Most strangers wouldn't bother. "I should have done them yellow with pink polka dots."

He grinned. "I dare you."

"I'm not *that* original," I said as I used the gray to extend my mountains to the bottom edge of the canvas.

"So you never told me what it is you do when you're not humoring your friend," Max said. "I'm going to cross painting off the list as well."

"Not a bartender or a painter. But hey, we've got time. If you keep guessing, I'm sure you'll come up with it eventually. What about you? What occupies all your waking hours?"

"Oh, so I have to tell you straight out, and you're making me guess?"

"Yes, I think so."

"Okay, I'm a librarian."

I laughed.

Max didn't.

Crap. "I'm sorry, I thought you were joking—like the whole bartender/painter thing. Are you really a librarian?"

"I will be when I finish school. Right now I just work in a library."

"That's really cool," I said.

"No, it's not. You laughed! You can't pretend you think it's cool now!"

"I thought it was part of the game. I wouldn't have laughed if I had known. Honest."

"Sure."

"I love books," I protested. "What could be better than to be surrounded by books all day?"

"It's not all day. I also write screenplays, but I haven't sold any yet."

"Wow, that really is cool."

"Right now I'm writing one about a guy who goes on lots of first dates. Girls seem to really like him until he tells them he's a librarian, and then they lose interest."

I laughed. "It sounds like a comedy."

"I'll let you know."

Chapter Thirteen

THE SERVER FINALLY RETURNED WITH the mayonnaise.

"Thank you," I said. "And I'm sorry—he's weird," I said, pointing to Max.

"You wound me," Max said. He picked up a french fry and dipped it in the mayo. "Try this," he said, handing it to me.

I stared at it for a minute as though it might be toxic.

"If you take as long to eat that as you did to paint the triangles, we'll still be here for the next class tomorrow."

I took a bite. "As much as it pains me to say this, it's actually not bad."

"Ha," he shouted.

"It's still weird," I said quickly. "And if I ate my fries like this, I'd weigh a thousand pounds."

"But you like it."

"I like it," I conceded. "But I'm going back to ketchup."

"As long as I know I'm right."

We went back to painting. I was beginning to think I had the triangle situation under control.

"Tell me about this guy you broke up with," Max said.

Suddenly triangles seemed like the least of my troubles.

"Unless you'd rather not," he added quickly when I didn't reply.

"Why do you want to know?" I asked while I considered how to begin with the tree trunks Max was effortlessly placing in the forefront of the painting.

"I'm a student of human behavior," he said.

"Sure you are."

"Maybe my motives aren't quite so noble. You're cute, and I'm curious."

I knew I was blushing, and I told myself not to, which only made my cheeks get hotter. "I'm not cute," I said, recklessly planting a tree because it was easier than looking at Max.

"Don't be so modest."

"Can we talk about something else?"

"If I promise to stop saying you're cute, will you tell me about this guy who wasn't good enough for you?"

I quickly did another tree, which was way too close to the first one. For at least the five hundredth time, I wished I had an eraser, but did it really matter? After all, it wasn't like this was going on anyone's wall when I was finished. "*He* dumped me." I scrubbed my brush around in the paint and added two more trees. Trees were addictive. Once you started, you couldn't have enough. Or maybe I was just uncomfortable with the direction this conversation was headed.

"I'm sorry," Max said. His voice was soft and kind and suddenly hard to hear over the music. "It never occurred to me that he might have dumped you, or I wouldn't have brought it up. I'm sorry," he repeated.

"Why did you assume I was the one who broke up with him?"

He gestured with his brush. "Look at you. Who would break up with you?"

"Stop."

"What?"

"You're being silly," I said. I focused on adding more trees. My picture was starting to look less and less like the one the instructor was painting. I definitely wouldn't win any prizes tonight, but it was too late to turn back now, and the soon-to-be forest was strangely comforting. I found myself unexpectedly pleased with it. "I remember reading a story once about a man who painted the same thing over and over again his whole life," I said, trying to distract him from our current conversation. "Maybe my thing is trees."

"I always say you can never have too many trees," Max said. "Thank you."

"But back to this breakup business. I'm being serious. You're cute, and you're funny. You like ginger ale, and you paint one heck of a tree." I looked at Max, and I could tell he really was being serious. "Who would break up with you? You're perfect."

"How can you say that? You've known me for exactly"—I stopped and glanced at my phone—"fifty-eight minutes," I said.

"Sometimes it doesn't take years or even months to find out that you click with someone. Sometimes it happens like *that*," he said, snapping his fingers loudly.

It was a nice moment. I held my breath while I mentally wrapped it up in a bow to admire it later.

"I've always wanted to be able to snap my fingers like that," I said. "Maybe you could teach me."

Trust me to ruin it.

"When you can paint trees like that, you don't need to snap to get people's attention," Max said. "Maybe you could teach me."

How did he know the perfect answer?

I glanced at Max's trees, which I now realized were infinitely better than mine and instantly felt deflated. What could I possibly teach him?

What was I doing? I wanted Colby, not a stranger I'd met an hour ago. If Colby walked in now, I'd choose him in a second.

Wouldn't I?

Chapter Fourteen

Of course this was the moment the instructor appeared.

"Goodness, you seem to have gotten carried away," she commented when she saw my expanding forest.

"I know. I think trees are the only thing I can do," I said.

"You might be surprised, but it never hurts to play to your strengths. Go where the brush leads you," she said. She walked farther down the row. When I looked back at Max, he was sticking his lower lip out, pouting. It was adorable.

"What is this about?" I asked, using my brush in the air to paint an imaginary circle around his sulky face.

"She didn't say anything about *my* trees."

"That's because your trees are perfect, Max," Elle said. I jumped. I hadn't realized she was standing behind us.

"What do you mean?" Max asked.

"The instructor only comments on the painters who need encouragement. She doesn't bother with the people who know what they're doing," she said.

I stuck my tongue out at her. "Mean," I said.

"I don't think that's it at all," Max said. "Cass's trees are obviously much nicer than mine."

Elle howled, startling the people sitting next to us. "Your trees might be flawless, but your lying needs work," she said.

My brush darted out and painted a spot on her arm before I could stop it.

"Oh, you'll pay for that," Elle said.

"I'm not worried."

"If you'll excuse me, I have to get back to my masterpiece," she said before returning to her spot around the corner.

"Trees are hungry work," Max said. "I think I'll order dessert. Would you like some?"

My stomach was still a little growly, but I couldn't tell if it was painting nerves or genuine hunger. "After those gourmet fries, I'm stuffed."

Max frowned. "Who says you have to be hungry to eat dessert?"

I laughed.

"Besides, I promised to buy you dessert if you painted your triangles like a good girl."

"Yeah, but I didn't paint them at the prospect of a free pastry. I only did it out of fear of the approaching instructor."

"Now I have to buy you two desserts—one for triangles and one for honesty."

"You don't have to buy me anything. I'm very busy painting trees."

"I think she's moving on to the sunset."

I had completely missed the sunset tutorial, but Max was right. "See? I'm already too far behind to eat dessert." I reached over with my brush and painted a dot on his hand.

"I thought you didn't like painting," he said.

"Painting people is more fun than painting pictures."

Max leaned over and took my hand, holding it in place while he painted a smiley face on it. His hand was warm, and I found myself hoping he'd paint an entire mural on my arm. "You're right; that is fun."

He let go of my hand, and I could still feel the impression of his fingers. It was pleasant, and I wondered how long the feeling would hang around.

Max caught the eye of the server, who headed in our direction. She was probably terrified at the prospect of what we might order next. "Last chance," he said.

The ghost of his fingers still tingled on my hand. I shook my head. "I'm fine."

"We'll see," he said.

Chapter Fifteen

"Is that key lime pie?" I asked. I had a soft spot for pie, and key lime was at the top of the list. I couldn't believe Max chose it. If I believed in signs, I'd be a little weirded out right now.

Max smiled. "I thought you didn't want any dessert."

"I don't. It was only a question. I'm showing an interest in something you're interested in."

"I see. Well, that's very polite of you." He scooped up a spoonful and ate it, closing his eyes while he chewed.

The nice thing about his eyes being closed was it gave me the opportunity to study him more closely, which I took full advantage of. Max was about as completely opposite Colby as I could imagine. Where Colby was dark and tanned, Max was ginger with the kind of pale, freckled skin that was wasted on a man. Pity I only had about five seconds to make my observations.

"Oh. Wow. This is delicious," he said, his eyes opening as he savored another spoonful.

My mouth started watering. "I'm happy for you."

"I don't suppose you'd like a bite. I asked for two spoons," he said, gesturing to the plate.

"I shouldn't let myself get distracted . . . from the trees," I said.

"But there are two spoons," he repeated.

"Well, I wouldn't want the second one to feel neglected." I picked up the spoon and took a bite. "Mmmm. Now that's true love," I said with my mouth full.

Max choked. "Pardon?"

"Key lime pie. It's my favorite," I explained. I didn't want Max to think I was some crazy girl who would fall head over heels for anyone who gave her a smidgen of pie. He probably thought I was flirting with him. Maybe I was, but why? To prove I could? That was a pretty low thing to do, even if I was a girl who'd recently been dumped and was looking for validation.

"I'll order another slice for you," he said.

Suddenly I felt silly about Max buying me anything, even a piece of pie. I didn't even know him. "I'm okay."

"Have more of mine, then." He pushed the plate toward me.

"Really, I'm good."

"But you said it's your favorite."

"It's delicious," I admitted. "But, no, thanks."

"Why can't you admit you want some?"

"Because I don't," I said.

"Okay. Just trying to be a gentleman." While Max ate the rest of the pie with the gusto of a five-year-old, with the taste of lime on my tongue, I painted my sun high in the sky instead of setting over the mountains. I kicked myself for being so stubborn. Part of me knew I was being ridiculous. It was a piece of pie, for heaven's sake, and Max seemed like a nice guy. But he'd bought me a drink, and already he wanted to move on to pie? What was next? Dinner? A movie? It was too soon. I wasn't ready.

"I want everyone to take a fifteen-minute break. Go for a walk, see some of the other paintings, enjoy dessert," the instructor said. Max smiled at me as he licked his spoon. I glared at him. "Rest your eyes for a minute. When you come back, we'll put leaves on the trees."

I got up. "I'm going for a walk," I announced.

"I'll join you," Elle said.

Chapter Sixteen

"I'm ready to go now," I said when we were out of the room.

"No, you're not," Elle said.

"You promised! You said that if I gave it a chance and still wanted to leave, we would."

I followed Elle to the restroom, and we went inside and sat on a little couch by the door. "Okay, why are you having a meltdown about a piece of pie?"

I stared at her. "Can you hear *everything* we're saying?"

"You like him," she said, ignoring my question.

"No, I don't."

"You do. I can tell. Why are you pushing him away?"

"I just met him. He could be a serial killer for all we know."

"This is about Colby, isn't it?" she said.

"Max is a stranger," I repeated. "I don't know anything about him. He bought me a drink, and now he wants to buy me pie? Don't you think that's a little fast?"

"Oh no! Ginger ale and a slice of pie." Elle gasped. "Now there's a man with sinister motives."

"You know what I mean. He could be a total creep."

"But he seems like a nice guy, right?"

I shrugged.

"Well, maybe you should trust your gut. Three months with Colby wasn't enough to know him, was it?"

"Yes. Exactly. I thought I was in love with Colby, and look where it got me. I'm certainly not going to trust my feelings about someone after two hours when I couldn't even get it right after three months."

"So this *is* about Colby."

I sighed. "Yes, this is about Colby. It's too soon. I'm not ready to give up on us yet."

"Cass . . ."

"He could still change his mind. Maybe he needs some time. I could try harder."

"I told Colby to come here tonight," Elle blurted.

My mouth dropped open, and my eyes darted around as though I expected him to be lurking in a corner of the ladies room. "What? Why? Why would you do that?"

"I told him you would be here and if he wanted to fix things, he should come."

"But you hate Colby."

"I hate the way he treated you. But I know that you love him, or at least you thought you loved him, and I want you to be happy."

My heart felt like it was getting bruised banging against my rib cage. Everything depended on this. "What did he say?" My voice was barely above a whisper, and I could feel the tears waiting to pounce like a trained assassin.

"Basically the same thing he said in your note, only I didn't know there was a note when I talked to him. He's very lucky to be alive."

I gave Elle a small laugh, but the assassin tears quickly took over.

"Look, I'm not saying this Max guy will turn out to be anything special. Most of them aren't. Like, 99.5 percent of them aren't," she said.

I rolled my eyes.

"But you should give it a chance. Don't waste your time waiting around for someone who isn't coming back."

I stood up and grabbed several tissues from the box on the counter. "You're a good friend," I said.

"Remember that when I need someone to bail me out of jail."

My laugh was genuine this time. "It's going to happen one day, isn't it?"

Elle pulled the Magic 8 ball out of her bag and shook it. "Signs point to yes."

I splashed some water on my face and blotted it dry with a paper towel.

"Are you ready to leave?" Elle asked.

There was a hollowness inside me, like someone had plucked out Colby and the hope of reconciliation so completely that only the memory of wanting him was left. The spot was still tender, but there was no gaping maw of regret. It seemed strange that a couple of hours ago I was waiting around in my little black dress, still harboring the delusion that he'd come around eventually. Maybe it had something to do with the week I'd spent mulling over the possible death of our relationship, but the fact that I'd skipped so quickly over the other stages of loss and gone straight to acceptance made me question if I'd ever really loved him in the first place. I suppose it was possible that I only loved the idea of telling someone I loved them.

"Not yet. There are still trees to paint," I said, squaring my shoulders.

"Leaves," Elle corrected.

"Whatever. You paint your thing. I'll paint mine."

We walked out of the bathroom together. "Why don't you just ask Max if he's in a relationship?" Elle asked.

"No! That's so awkward. I'd feel pathetic."

"If you don't ask him, I will."

I punched her in the arm. "You. Wouldn't. Dare."

She punched me back harder. "Believe me; it would be much better if you figured out a way to ask him."

I shook my head. "You won't do it. You're not that crazy."

"Wanna bet? I'll give you another thirty minutes to work it into the conversation, but don't say I didn't warn you."

"You're an evil genius, but you neglected one little detail. What's to stop me from leaving now?"

"You said it yourself—there are still leaves to paint."

"Trees."

"Whatever." Elle grinned. "Plus, I have the keys."

Chapter Seventeen

When I got back, Max's chair was empty. I was a little relieved. I hoped my red eyes would be gone by the time he returned. But as I sat and started to paint yet more unauthorized trees, I found I missed him. It was nice to talk and joke around with someone I wasn't trying to impress, for a change. I resolved that in the future I would stop trying to be who I thought guys wanted me to be and just be myself, a feat easier said than done. Elle liked the real me, and Max appeared to be on board, so maybe other people would like it too. And on that note, I decided I wanted blossoms in my trees instead of leaves.

I cleaned my brush in the water before covering it thoroughly in white paint. Since I had no idea how to paint blossoms (or leaves, for that matter), I made quick dabs with my brush in a sort of stabbing motion, like a pogo stick. I was so pleased with them that after a while I started mixing red and white paint for pink blossoms.

"Oh no, have I been gone that long?" Max asked. His face was red, and I fought the bizarre impulse to ask if he'd been crying too.

"Have you been outside?" I asked incredulously.

"Yes."

"When the instructor suggested you go for a walk, I don't think she meant it literally. It must be below zero out there. What were you thinking?"

Max took off his coat and blew on his hands to warm them up. "You were gone a while. I thought maybe you weren't coming back."

"You were looking for me?"

He nodded. "I looked all over. Where were you?"

I laughed. I couldn't help it. "We were in the one place you'd never find us—the restroom."

"Oh. Well, I couldn't exactly look in there, could I? I notice you weren't too worried about me disappearing."

"Hey! Believe it or not, I missed you."

"Says the girl who's very calmly painting blossoms on her trees. Except I thought we were supposed to be painting leaves."

"I'm branching out. Get it—branching, trees?"

Max laughed, which was generous given the quality of the joke.

"Sorry, bad pun. Mine are still deciding if they want to be leaves when they grow up."

"So you're an existentialist, minimalist painter. It just gets better." Max sat and started painting green and yellow leaves that looked so pretty I almost wished I'd done what I was told instead of making it up as I went along.

"I'm not a painter at all," I said.

"Of course you are. More importantly, you're a painter who doesn't follow the crowd. That makes you an artist."

"Elle was right. You are a bad liar."

"You still haven't told me what your real job is," Max said.

"You're welcome to as many guesses as you'd like."

"Uh, you're a teacher."

"Nope. I'd be terrible at that."

"Really, why?"

"I just would," I said.

"Oh, no, you're not getting off that easily. This is the interesting part."

I thought for a minute. "Maybe I'm afraid of being wrong. And large packs of children scare me."

Max laughed. "Fair enough. So, not a teacher. How about a nurse?"

"Ugh. I'd rather be a teacher."

"Because?"

"I don't have that much patience with people." Why did I want to be so honest with Max? Being yourself was one thing. Throwing yourself under the bus was another.

"An engineer?"

"Is that supposed to be funny?"

"It was a serious guess!"

"Do I look like an engineer to you?"

"You could be. Cute girls can be engineers too."

I stared at him. "I can't even paint a straight triangle."

"Good point."

"Feel free to stop anytime," I said.

"I'm no quitter. I won't stop until I guess it."

"Famous last words."

"Uh, butcher?" he asked.

"Gross."

"Baker?"

"I burn things in the kitchen."

"Candlestick maker?"

I paused as though I was considering the possibility. "I did make a candle once in elementary school, but no."

"I'm afraid we'll run out of canvas before I run out of guesses."

"Do you give up?"

"I never give up," he said firmly.

"She's a veterinary assistant," a voice said from across the table.

"Elle!" we said simultaneously.

"I'm sorry, but it was like watching the world's longest game of charades, and I couldn't take it anymore," she said. "Now we can all move on."

"You're a vet?" Max asked.

"An assistant, but that's the plan."

"You like animals?"

"I love animals." I smiled at him. "They're much better than people, for the most part. I've never met an animal I didn't like."

"What about snakes? They seem pretty unlikable."

"I love snakes," I cooed. "I had a pet snake when I was a little girl. Well, it wasn't a real pet. It was just a grass snake I found in the yard. My mom grounded me for a week when she found out I'd been keeping it in the house."

"Did she make you let it go?"

I shook my head, grinning. "My brother tattled on me, but when she went into my room to get rid of it, we couldn't find it. She wanted to move."

Max shuddered. "Your mother seems like a very sensible woman."

Chapter Eighteen

"Okay," Chelly said. "Who's ready to do the pond?"

"Say what now?" I said to Max.

"We're going to do the pond," he said, dipping his brush in the blue and watching Chelly go to work.

"What pond? Since when is there a pond?"

"What did you think the blue was for?" Max asked. I could tell he was making a valiant struggle not to laugh.

"I don't know. Clouds?"

"Clouds! There you go; you can do clouds. You've been doing your own thing all along, so why not have some clouds?"

"There isn't room for clouds. The trees have completely taken over."

"There is a definite pond. Didn't you see the picture when you signed up?"

"I didn't sign up. I didn't even know we were coming here until we arrived, and I only agreed to leave the house because *she* promised me fish," I said, pointing at Elle.

"Like fish and chips?" Max asked.

"No, goldfish. Why would you think I meant fish and chips?"

He gave me a strange look. "Why would I think you meant goldfish?"

"Never mind. There's no way I can do a pond," I said.

"Of course you can. You said you couldn't do the triangles either, and look how far you've come."

"I meant I don't have any room for a pond. My whole canvas is full of trees!"

"Yes, that could be a problem," Max said.

I heard Elle snicker.

"Are you laughing over there?" I said loudly.

"Maybe this will teach you to follow directions," she said.

"I regret nothing! I love my trees. We were fine before all of this pond talk."

"Don't worry about it. Your picture is fine the way it is," Max said.

"No, I should have listened."

"But you just said you didn't care about the pond."

"That was big talk for Elle. When you have a friend like her, you have to own your choices, otherwise she'll think you screwed up. But everyone else is going to have a nice painting to take home, and I'll have a jumble of trees."

"Don't you get it? Yours is better than all of ours. We're all following orders, and you're thinking for yourself."

"You're only trying to make me feel better," I said.

Max sighed as though he was trying to explain algebra to a dog. "If this was for a class and you were being graded, you might have a point. There's something to be said for being able to follow directions. But this is supposed to be fun. You should go back to painting what you like. At least you were having a good time."

I was silent for a minute while I watched Max shape his pond in the space on the canvas that had been left open specifically for that purpose. When we'd arrived earlier, I'd been too nervous to pay much attention to the picture at the front, but now it seemed obvious. As much as I wanted a pond now, I couldn't see any way to make it work, short of painting it over the trees, and I liked them too much. Max was right. I'd rather paint it my way and enjoy doing it than stress over trying to make it like the model.

I watched Max paint his pond instead, trying to make the ripples on the surface of the water. He wasn't very good at it, which made me feel a little bit better since he seemed overly good at everything else he'd tried.

"Ponds are harder than they look," he said finally.

"I think you did great. And now your woodland animals won't get thirsty."

Max laughed. "If the pond was this difficult, I can't imagine painting the animals."

"Don't worry; they're imaginary," I assured him.

"Oh, good."

He continued to fiddle with the water, using his brush in different ways to try to make the ripples look more real.

"Are there goldfish in your pond?" I asked.

"Of course."

"I can't see them."

"That's because they're imaginary goldfish."

I nodded. "That makes sense."

Chapter Nineteen

WE WERE MOVING ON TO grasses. I watched as Chelly effortlessly flicked the brush near the trees, making grass that looked lifelike enough to leap off the canvas.

"Grass looks like the easiest thing yet," I said. "I definitely have room for grass."

"Go on, then. Give it a try," Max said.

"You first."

I watched as he mixed a little green and yellow together. He held his brush at the end like Chelly had instructed us before making the same flicking motions she had. In a few seconds, beautiful grass began to line the area around the trees.

I was jealous. "That looks like professional grass."

"Easy as pie," Max pronounced. "Can't go wrong. Your turn."

I thought trees were my thing, but maybe it was grass. I mixed the same colors together, held my brush the same way, and flicked it against the canvas in a way that was careless and controlled at the same time. But instead of professional grass, I got uneven clumps. So I dipped it in the paint and tried again with the same results. I growled.

"What's wrong?" Max asked. He was still adding grass that looked as though there should be cartoon bunnies playing in it.

"Grass is not my thing."

"But it's so easy!"

I glared at him.

"I think there's too much paint on your brush," he said quickly. "Maybe you should clean it off and try again."

Too much paint. That must be it. It was always the easiest solution that I never thought of, like when my cell phone screen froze and I tried every trick in the world to fix it before someone asked if I'd turned it off and on again. It worked every time. I rinsed out my brush and dried it with the paper towel before reapplying a small amount of paint. I held my breath and tried it again . . . with similar results. I was getting seriously frustrated.

"It still doesn't work! And you said grass is easy. What's wrong with me?"

Max took my brush and squinted at it. "I think it's your brush. You might have killed it with your enthusiasm over the blossoms."

"You're just saying that to make me feel better. I can't even paint grass."

"It has to be your brush. Anyone who can paint trees like that could conquer grass with one hand tied behind their back," he said. He was still adding more stellar grass. Some might say it was too much grass, but who could blame him? If you could do anything that well, why wouldn't you fill your whole canvas with it?

I continued trying various methods of painting grass, but either my brush was toast, or grass and I didn't mesh. I finally quit because it was ruining the trees, and they were the one thing I had going for me. I watched Max instead, who was concentrating on evenly distributing tall grass and short grass. He was biting his lip, and it was cute, and suddenly I realized I was staring at his lips, which led to wondering if he was a good kisser.

Elle popped up from behind her canvas, and I realized what she was doing a second before she actually did it. I gave her my don't-do-it-you'll-ruin-everything look, and she gave me her corresponding too-late-you-missed-your-chance-so-now-I-have-to look.

"Max, you seem like a nice enough guy," Elle said innocently. "You have great taste in dessert, you paint amazing . . . grass. Why aren't you in a relationship?"

"What makes you think I'm not?" he said.

Elle was taken aback. I don't think I'd ever seen someone throw her off her game before. "You're here by yourself," she said once she'd regained her composure.

"Yes, and I've been flirting with your friend all night," Max said, smiling at me.

My face was red; I could tell.

"Exactly, and she just got out of a relationship. I don't want her to get hurt," Elle said.

"Excuse me, I'm right here!" I said.

"Well, you can set your mind at ease because I'm not the kind of guy who flirts with random girls when I've got one waiting at home," Max said.

"That's all I needed to know. You may continue with your grass," Elle said, disappearing again behind her painting.

"That wasn't mortifying at all," I said.

"It's nice that you have someone looking out for you."

"It's none of her business. If I wanted to know your dating status, I would ask."

He looked hurt. "You didn't want to know?"

This conversation was quickly going from good to grand-prize award for awkward. I couldn't believe Elle had put me in this position. "What I meant was it's not my business any more than it is hers."

"What if I want it to be your business?" Max said, putting down his brush and facing me.

I had no idea what to say. My tongue was cemented to the roof of my mouth, and my brain was temporarily out of service.

"I'm single," Max said. "And in case you have any doubts, I've been throwing my best flirting at you all night."

He was staring at me so intently that I shouldn't have been surprised when he leaned over, closing the small space between us to kiss me. It was only a short kiss but enough for me to discover two things—one, it was different than kissing Colby. And two, I liked it. Where I'd enjoyed kissing Colby, and his skills had been perfectly adequate, it hadn't been exciting. I'd never thought about it at the time, but I was always the one kissing Colby. He never pursued me. So it was amazing being kissed by someone who wanted to kiss me.

My brain had conveniently timed out, so when Max pulled away and I remembered where we were, I was embarrassed.

"I shouldn't have done that. I'm an idiot," Max said.

"Why?"

"You just got out of a relationship. You said it yourself; you think you might get back together with him."

"His name is Colby," I said. I hadn't intended to say it out of nowhere like that. It just came out. Sometimes I had to imagine myself saying something brave multiple times before the words actually came out, but that had been effortless.

Max leaned in closer. "What did you say?"

"His name is Colby—the guy who broke up with me. His name is Colby, and we're definitely not getting back together."

"Hallelujah," Elle mumbled from the other side of the table.

I waited for the squall of tears, but they didn't come. Not even a hint of salt on the horizon.

"I'm sorry," Max said.

"Why are you sorry?" I asked.

"I'm not. I'm incredibly relieved and happy, but that didn't seem like the appropriate thing to say in this situation." He put his hand over mine and squeezed it, and everything was right with the world, at least momentarily.

I felt giddy and reckless, and I wondered what my painting would look like now if I started again with a blank canvas. I predicted it would be positively peppered with polka dots. I tried to remember if Colby and I had been like this at the beginning of our relationship. If we had, there was no memory of this feeling. I can't recall him ever grinning like Max when he held my hand. "As long as you're not sorry," I said.

Chapter Twenty

If only finishing my painting could be as easy as kissing Max.

I stared at my canvas. "Something is wrong with it."

"I think it's incredible," Max said. He had finally quit with his grass and returned to working on the perfect leaves.

"In theory, I think you should be looking at my picture if you want me to take your comment seriously."

"Sorry," Max said. He set his brush down and walked around my painting, studying it from every angle as though he was an art critic. "I think it's the mountains," he said finally. "The rest of the painting is so happy, but the mountains are bringing it down. Maybe you should have done the yellow with the pink polka dots."

"I think if I tried to paint yellow over the gray now, it would be hideous. This will have to do."

"The good news is there are so many trees that you can hardly see the mountains."

"True," I said. It was funny to see all the other paintings that were near copies of the one at the front of the room compared to mine. As long as I had tried to copy it, I hadn't had any fun, but as soon as I'd surrendered to my own vision, I'd started to enjoy myself. I was guessing the guy sitting next to me had a lot to do with the fun factor as well.

People were starting to pick up their canvases and head toward the door, and I was surprised to realize I didn't want the night to be over.

"Are you finished?" I asked Elle, who was still sitting on the other side of the table.

"I'm ready if you are," she said.

"I still haven't seen your painting. Let's have a look," I said.

She held up her painting, which was almost a carbon copy of the one at the front. "I had no idea you could paint like that!" I said.

She shrugged. "It's just copying. Anyone can copy some-thing." She almost looked bored. I held up my painting, and she smirked. "I mean *almost* anyone can copy something."

Max gave Elle a look of undisguised admiration. "You could be a forger."

"She's going to end up in jail eventually. Don't give her any ideas," I said.

Chelly stopped us on our way out. "Can I get a quick picture? For the website?" Her eyes landed on my painting, which had even more trees than the last time she'd commented on it. Then her gaze drifted away, and she smiled reassuringly, but I'm sure she was thinking, *Okay, maybe not* that *picture for the website.*

"Sure, why not?" Max said.

"Uh, maybe because my picture looks nothing like all the others," I whispered.

"If you'll all stand over there in front of the Paint Nite banner," Chelly said.

The three of us stood in an awkward clump, like strangers. I considered moving the painting to hide my face at the last minute so no one could recognize me.

"You be in the middle, Cass," Elle said. I moved over to stand between Max and her. I sort of hoped he'd sneak his arm around me, but that would have been difficult since we were all holding our paintings.

"Aaaaaand I'm getting my picture taken now. How did you manage to fit all the things that scare me into one evening?" I said to Elle through my forced grin.

"It's a gift."

"That's perfect," Chelly said. "Smile."

And it was over. I desperately wanted to ask Chelly for a copy of the picture since I might never see Max again after tonight. Elle must have been reading my mind though.

"I better get a picture too," she said, taking out her phone.

"Here, I'll take one of the two of you," Max offered.

Elle brushed him off. "I have a million pictures of us. Let me get one of you guys. Okay, get closer . . . closer . . ." She frowned. "Maybe you should put the paintings down."

I rolled my eyes. This was getting beyond embarrassing. I felt like Max and I were going to prom and Elle was my enthusiastic yet overbearing mother. "Just take the picture."

"Smile!" she said. So we did. And it was over. Again.

"Can I walk you ladies to your car?" Max asked.

I wasn't ready for the night to be over. Before we left the room, I wanted some sort of guarantee that I would see Max again. Instead, I said, "Of course."

Chapter Twenty-One

"WELL, THANK YOU FOR A wonderful evening," Max said. "This is for you." He gave me a white Styrofoam box. I handed it to Elle, and she put it in the trunk of her car with our canvases.

"Thank you. It was very nice to meet you," I said, cursing myself for the formality of my response. It sounded like we'd just completed a job interview. I might as well have shaken his hand and been done with it.

"I guess this is it," he said.

"Yup," I said. It was freezing cold outside, and Elle was already in the car with the engine running. I fought the urge to hop from one leg to the other to generate some heat. *Come on! Ask for my number, Max, or you'll never see me again!*

"Are you cold?"

I nodded my head so hard I thought it might come off.

Max held out his arms and moved toward me with a question in his eyes. I moved into his outstretched arms, and he hugged me. I buried my face in his neck. He smelled nice, like he'd just returned from walking through the forest I'd painted. "It was very nice to meet you too," he said in my ear.

He let me go and opened my door. I slid inside, my pulse racing from the hug but, at the same time, disappointed. I knew next to nothing about him, not even his last name. And it wasn't like we'd met at a restaurant or a bookstore where we would have a chance of running into each other again—not unless I started going to every Paint Nite in the valley.

"Drive safe," he said, closing my door.

Chapter Twenty-Two

I WATCHED HIM RUN BACK toward the building, presumably to retrieve his painting. He was gone.

"Well?" Elle said impatiently.

"Well, what?"

"You know what. What happened?"

"Nothing happened. He hugged me, and that was all."

"That can't be all. He liked you. He *kissed* you."

"Maybe it was just a crazy impulse."

"He liked you," she repeated. "I could tell."

"Even you have been known to be wrong on occasion. I'm going to need a copy of that picture," I said.

"Already sent it to you. And you're welcome." She grinned.

We hung around for a minute, but Max didn't immediately reappear, and I didn't want him to come out in an hour to find us still sitting here waiting. "Let's go," I said finally.

"Are you sure?"

"Yeah. I think I've had enough excitement for one night."

As we drove down the canyon and back to the city, it was quiet in the car. I don't know what Elle was thinking about, but I was lost in my thoughts of Max. I really thought he'd liked me too.

"That can't be it," Elle said again. "I refuse to believe that he'd let you go like that with no way to contact you." She brightened. "Maybe he went back inside to get your info from the instructor."

"Did she have any of my info?"

"Uh, no. Not even your last name because I bought the tickets. But she had my name. Maybe he'll get that and track you down through me."

"He's not a detective. If he wanted my number, he would have just asked. And unless I hang around up there hoping to see him again, *I'd* have to be a detective to track him down."

"A detective. You'd have to be a detective," Elle mused.

"Either you have an idea, or you're having a stroke."

"A detective looks for clues. Maybe he left you a clue. Think back to your conversation. Was there anything . . . clue-like?"

I concentrated for a minute before I realized how ridiculous the suggestion was. "There was no trail of breadcrumbs. Sorry."

Elle parked the car in front of my apartment and took the Magic 8 ball out of her bag. "Does Max want to see Cass again?" She shook it. "Without a doubt," she said smugly.

"For a guy who wants to see me again, he didn't make it very simple."

Elle popped the trunk, and I got out to retrieve my painting. There, sitting next to the canvas was the Styrofoam box. I'd completely forgotten about it. I opened it to find a slice of key lime pie—very thoughtful but basically not helpful. When I picked up the box, I noticed something taped to the bottom.

"A *clue*!" I yelled triumphantly.

"What are you screaming about?" Elle yelled back from the front seat.

I got back into the car. "There really is a clue."

"What is it?" she asked.

"A piece of key lime pie. That's what was in the box Max gave me when we were leaving. There's something taped to the bottom."

Elle rolled her eyes. "And you're only *now* thinking this might be significant? What does it say?" She sounded as though she was one step away from ripping it out of my hands and reading it herself.

I unfolded the note and scanned the contents. I couldn't help grinning.

"It's his phone number. He said he didn't want to ask for mine because I just got out of a relationship and he didn't know if I was ready."

"Imagine that—a decent guy. What are the chances? You should call him."

"I can't call him now! I just saw him. He'd think I was crazy."

"He gave you his number. Doesn't that imply he wants you to call him?"

"Yeah, eventually. If I call him now, it seems so desperate."

"Well, at least text him," she said.

"I'll do it tomorrow. And where are my fish?"

Elle clicked her tongue as she shook her head. "Walmart, darling. Your fish are at Walmart."

"I *knew* it!"

"Don't fret. I've given you something much better. All you have to do is call him."

I went inside and gave George salad. I liked to think she was happy to see me, but she was probably more excited about the lettuce. Then I ate the pie while I flipped through TV channels. I lasted ten whole minutes before I texted Max. *Thank you for the pie.*

Ugh. I should have taken some time to carefully compose my text. Like painting, there was no eraser for texting. I guess it could have been worse. I didn't know what to say, but "Thank you for the pie" seemed less threatening than "I know we just met, but I can't stop thinking about you." Maybe I should have sent him a snatch of poetry. A librarian would like that, right? Something about his epic lips, perhaps?

My text alert sounded, and I was almost too nervous to look at it.

I can't believe it took you this long to text me! I obviously didn't make the same impression on you that you did on me. ;)

I was giddier reading that text than any other in recent memory. *I barely found your clue. The pie was in the trunk. I probably should have waited until tomorrow to text you anyway.*

Why?

I don't know. This seems incredibly desperate on my part.

Cass, you're talking to a guy who definitely would have kept kissing you tonight if he'd been sure you were ready. Who's the desperate one now?

The idea that Max was still thinking about kissing me made me shiver. Kissing Colby had been nice, but I got the impression that kissing Max, really kissing him, might be life changing.

This is silly, I told myself. *You only met this guy tonight. He's nice to you and shows an interest in your life and buys you pie, and suddenly you're thinking of jumping back into a relationship?*

Yes. It might be crazy, but yes, I was.

I feel guilty, I texted. *You bought me a drink and pie, and I didn't get you anything. How about I buy you dinner this week, and we can talk about this kissing prospect?* I debated pushing send before I decided to take a chance. It seemed like an eternity before his response arrived.

Why not? I wouldn't let any other girl buy me dinner, but you are different. You paint yellow mountains with pink polka dots. You wanna hear a secret?

I realized I was smiling, one of those grins that almost hurt my face. *I love secrets.*

I've always wanted to date a rebel.

It was too soon to be sure, but I was pretty certain that if I asked Elle's Magic 8 ball if my spell of tears was over, it would say the outlook was good.

About the Author

AUBREY MACE LIVES IN SANDY, Utah. She has five published novels: *Spare Change*, which won the Whitney Award for Best Romance; *My Fairy Grandmother*; *Santa Maybe*, nominated for a Whitney Award for Best Romance; *Before the Clock Strikes Thirty*; and *Love on a Whim*. She also has a novella, "The Science of Sentiment" in the Timeless Romance Anthology Spring Vacation Collection.

When she isn't at her day job or writing, Aubrey enjoys cooking, attempting to grow things, traveling, reading, and spending time with her family. She also likes dark chocolate, birds, IKEA, and British comedy, in no particular order.

Website: www.aubreymace.com
Twitter: @AubreyMace
Facebook: Aubrey Mace

AUBREY MACE HAS ALSO WRITTEN

Before the Clock Strikes Thirty
Love on a Whim